THE FAE Pₐ   S

THE PACIFIC PRINCESSES: BOOK 2

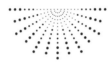

EKTAA BALI

BLUE MOON RISING PUBLISHING

Print ISBN: 9780648983057

E-book ISBN: 9780648983040

The author acknowledges the Traditional Custodians of the land where this novel was written and based. We acknowledge their connections to land, sea and community. We pay our respects to their elders past and present and extend that respect to all Aboriginal and Torres Strait Islander peoples today.

For Vidya, the sweetest, most caring little girl I know.

&

For my Nani, Subbhya Wati, for teaching me that when you speak, you should always speak with love.

THE FAE PRINCESS

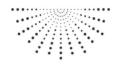

THE BOOK OF THE FAE

When the world was new, it slept in the shadow womb of the universe. Then fire came and made things move. Then, water cooled the earth. As time passed, the earth arose from the sea, and the Flower of Awakening saw the light and finally, her song could be heard through the crisp air. The Fae awoke and sprung from the wet earth, with hearts that were whole and pure. When they spoke the language of the earth, and sung its song, the trees and flowers listened and grew tall. The Fae and land were one, and until the end of time, they would sing their songs and watch over the earth and keep it safe. For where there is magic and power, there is a fine and precious balance that must be kept.

—The Book of the Fae, Queen Mab the First, 3333 B.C.

King Farrion of the Eastern Bushland Fae strode through the ancient forest. He had travelled for seven days and seven nights through thunder and rain, fire and dangerous caverns to get to this place. A place not visited by any living soul except he and the Fae Kings and Queens before him.

Access to the Valley of Old was granted only to deserving Fae royalty. There was too much power here and too much to be lost to allow anyone but the most worthy to walk through. King Farrion had only been here twice before. It was only to be used in times of greatest need where wisest of council was required.

For two weeks now, King Farrion had felt something growing within him. A feeling of dread so awful it made him break out into a cold sweat in the middle of the night. He had never felt anything like it. Sinister and unrelenting, it had made him think of decaying plants, rotten fruit, and sick animals. And to the Fae, beings of fertility and health, this was the worst possible thing he could imagine. He could not understand where it was coming from, or why. All he knew was that feeling was growing. It had started within and it was now all around him. Throughout his sky palace and all through the Fae forest. Something was very, very wrong, and he needed advice. Advice from those who knew All. If anyone could help him, these beings would.

Everything in this forest was unspeakably huge. King Farrion was a large Fae, made of heavy muscle, but he felt like a tiny insect walking through this ancient place, and he felt its magic in his soul. This is how he knew he was in the right place. It was always different, getting to the Valley of Old. The magic that made this place was rooted in the heart of secret magic of the Fae so deeply that it was a secret folded within other secrets.

King Farrion walked amongst the gigantic gum trees, including the eucalypts, and felt his own heart sing. As guardian of the eucalyptus trees, they called out to him so lovingly that despite his haste to keep moving, he let himself run his hands against their trunks as he passed.

It would take a full minute to walk around the base of these trees, he marvelled. They had been brought here from another place and time, in an era remembered by none. None, that is, except for those who lived here.

This was the home of the Old Ones.

Farrion saw the clearing through the trees. This was it. The sacred meeting point for the Fae and the Old Ones. He paused in the line of trees bordering the clearing and took a deep breath, reaching for the vial he had kept safe on a cord around his neck.

He stepped out into the clearing in front of a small flat rock and cleared his throat. Clutching the glass vial, he spoke the words his forefathers had handed down to him.

"Old ones," he called. "King Farrion of the Eastern Bushland Fae humbly requests your aid and counsel. Please heed my call."

It began as a rumble in the distance. Farrion felt the land beneath him vibrate.

Trying to still his pounding heart, he listened to the deep *boom* of many heavy footsteps getting closer and closer.

The trees surrounding the clearing rustled, and all at once—the Old Ones took their spots, forming a large semi-circle before him.

There were seven of them, and they were huge.

Towering above him, Farrion craned his head upward to peer respectfully at them all as they looked down at him with assessing, knowing eyes.

No one knew their names, they were only known by their titles. They were the gigantic ancestors of the animals that currently roamed the Australian continent. The megafauna. These were the only ones left.

King Farrion acknowledged them one by one with his eyes, as his father had taught him.

The Great Echidna was as big as a hippopotamus, her long spikes glinting dangerously in the low light.

The Great Platypus, as large as a bull, gazed pleasantly back at him.

The Great Australian Lion was twice the size of lions normally found in African jungles and majestically sat on his hind legs.

The Great Wombat was as large as any elephant Farrion had seen and stood serenely still.

The Great Kangaroo stood taller than the height of two grown men standing on top of each other, intimidating with his strong, muscular chest.

The Thunderbird was taller still, with his extraordinarily long neck, and powerful muscular legs.

The Great Python, well over ten metres long, was mostly coiled, with his head raised, tasting the air with his tongue.

Farrion gulped under their heavy gazes. He took a steadying breath that moved his shoulders slightly and held out his glass vial. In it, sat a tiny shining crystal.

"Old ones, I present my offering. A crystallised tear of a Fae seeing the love of his life return to him."

He bent down and with both hands set it on the flat rock in front of him.

"This is a most precious gift, Farrion," said the Great Kangaroo in a deep, resonant voice. "What is it that ails you?"

"I… feel something in the air. Something dark. I cannot quite place it. I have never felt this before. It is sinister and unwavering. Haunting."

A wind blew through the clearing, and Farrion was

reassured by the familiar smell of the eucalypts. His beating heart slowed, and spoke his mind.

"I think something is coming for the Fae. I sense a change in the air and… in myself."

"This is troubling," came the mild voice of the Great Echidna. "Are you sure it is not just some unrest in the Fae forest?"

Farrion shook his head slowly at her. "No, I—"

He paused. This thing he had been thinking—too fearful to say out loud for many days now needed to be said. He could not keep it in the dark any longer. They needed to know.

"There is one more thing."

He took a deep breath.

"I feel the power of the Fae weakening."

For the first time in his memory, Farrion saw the Old Ones exchange uncomfortable glances.

"This is troubling news, Farrion," hissed the Great Python.

"Things begin…" droned the Great Wombat. "And so, things must also end."

Silence. Farrion frowned. Did he mean that this meant the power of the Fae was ending? That they would be gone? No, he couldn't possibly mean that. The line of the Fae could not end with him. He wouldn't allow it.

"There must be a source," he said quickly. "Some reason for it that I can stop—"

"Then," interrupted the Great Python, "if there is a cause, you must find it and create a solution."

The same power that kept the Fae alive was the

same power that kept the earth alive. The same power that kept the Old Ones alive. Farrion spread his hands out in front of him.

"The power of the Fae is tied to the land. The very earth itself. How could anything tamper with that?"

"Summer may follow spring," boomed the Great Thunderbird. "But winter must follow autumn."

What on earth does that mean? Farrion thought, astounded. He had expected some type of answer, or show of support, not riddles telling him this was as natural as the seasons!

"I do not know what to do," was all he could say.

"We have seen every age, Farrion," said the Great Echidna. "There comes a time in every age where a King's rule is challenged. You must look deep within to find the heart of what it means to be Fae. And there you will find your answer."

Farrion gaped at her and then remembered who he was speaking to and closed his mouth.

"The very existence of the Fae is being challenged, Old one. This is a problem I do not believe the Fae have ever seen before."

"There was one time," boomed the Great Thunderbird. "A time even none here remember."

A time before the Old Ones themselves? This talking in riddles was not helping. His people were at risk. Everything was at risk.

"I can feel it, Old Ones. I feel something coming. Something big. Something that seeks to bring down the Fae."

There was silence.

Then the Great Kangaroo spoke in a voice that Farrion felt in his bones.

"This tells me one thing, Farrion."

Farrion waited, holding his breath.

"That you must prepare for war."

1

THE FIRST DAY OF SPRING

To be Fae is to hear the whispers of trees as one would hear their own thoughts. It is to feel the earth beneath your feet as one would feel their own heartbeat. It is to see the dance of all the things that make up the world and know that dance, dances within you.

—The Book of the Fae, Queen Mab the First, 3333 B.C.

Deep in the bushland off the Eastern Australian coast, behind a door hidden inside a eucalyptus tree, lies the Kingdom of Eastern Bushland Fae. This is just one of the many hidden kingdoms of the world. Each Fae kingdom differs greatly from the others, and this particular one is marked by its magnificent city in the sky.

Through the tree-portal, you will find yourself in a lush green forest like no other. This is the Fae Forest, and the deeper you wander, the stranger and more tricksy the creatures and plants become. There are goblins who will steal your nose, trees with long fingers that will snatch bags from unsuspecting travellers, and worst still are the cunning spirits who pretend to help you but will only lead you deeper into danger.

If you are lucky enough to find the path that leads out of the forest, you will find that you cannot continue any further. In front of you is the edge of a cliff. The drop is so sudden that many an unknowing traveller falls right off, down into the depths of the Bottomless Sky. For in this realm, below the cliff, there is no land at all. Fall into the Bottomless Sky, and you might very well be falling until the end of time.

But if you are clever enough not to fall, right in front of you, in the middle of the sky, upon a heavy white cloud, you will see the fabled Fae City. The first thing you will see is a garden path leading up to the Royal Palace. It is a beauty of pure silver spires that plunge into the blue sky, magnificent stone turrets, and golden staircases. Behind the palace lies the famous Fae greenhouses where the King and Queen keep the most dangerous and valuable plants known on the earth, guarded by trained captains of the Fae Guard.

Behind the greenhouses and down a long, paved path lies the Fae city where the buildings, shops, and homes of the Fae are built in and around tall trees full of old magic.

* * *

On the crisp morning of September the 1st, also the first day of the Australian spring, every Fae of the Eastern Bushland kingdom was gathered on the neat green lawn in front of the palace, blinking at each other through the blue-grey light before the dawn arrived.

They swayed slowly, like sleepy bees, in time to the twinkling music of the flute and *thump thud thump* of tiny drums being played by Fae musicians. Each green eyed, brown face was turned toward the sky, their patient gazes upon the treetops of the Fae forest. They were waiting for the sun to rise above the trees, because for the Fae, the first dawn of spring was a sacred day.

The Fae are a colourful community, because even though they each have the same forest green eyes and skin the colour of rich bark, their wings and hair are of a colour unique to them. Rich blues, light greens, bright yellows, and glowing pinks; every colour imaginable was dotted throughout the crowd, making the group look very much like a collection of flowers swaying gently in a breeze.

Parents rocked on the spot with yawning children, babies were tightly wrapped in colourful blankets to protect delicate wings, but each Fae above the age of seven also held something equally precious in their hands.

The Fae are the guardians of the plants, and so each Fae is born linked to their own guardian species of plant, their companions for life. It is like having best friends who you can tell whenever they are sad or happy, hungry, or thirsty. And in return for the loving care, the plant gives the Fae special powers. Ghost berries made the Fae invisible to human eyes, Bilberries made them see in the dark like it was day, and Eucalyptus leaves had healing properties. The collection of herbs, flowers, and plants made the morning air smell like roses, eucalyptus, and rosemary, and the Fae breathed in that smell like it was life itself, for, to them, that's exactly what their plants were.

At the front of the group there was a slight movement as King Farrion slipped unnoticed into the crowd next to his wife. As he stroked his deep blue beard, the pink-winged Queen Salote turned to him with a sigh of relief.

"Oh, thank the earth you're back, Farrion," she whispered urgently, tugging on his arm. "I was so worried."

Farrion smiled lovingly at his wife and placed the Eucalyptus branch he was holding into his jacket pocket. He leaned toward her with a finger outstretched and gently tugged on the blanket of the small bundle in her arms. The tiny newborn Princess Mahiya squirmed in her sleep, a tiny tuft of peach coloured hair peeking out. She strained in her blankets, and before the Queen could warn the King, a loud *squelch* came from her diaper, followed by a tiny spark of orange-red flame that flew out of her nose. Both the King and Queen twitched in surprise, casting each other a wary look. Since her birth three weeks ago, the newborn Princess had erupted sparks at random times, usually with a sneeze or a fart. The Fae were creatures of the earth, not fire, and the reason their new Princess was setting small fires was yet to be discovered.

And there is another thought Farrion, bemused. *One more mystery to be solved.*

"I am perfectly well, my queen," he murmured. "But there will be much to talk about after the sun arrives."

The Queen looked into the King's weary face and nodded, a small crease forming between her pink brows. As the King's wife, it was her job as Queen to rule over the Fae city and its people, while it was his job to rule over the Fae forest, the animals, and protect the surrounding realms. She had felt the waning of the Fae magic in her people, just as he had over the last few weeks, and she could tell he had learned something in his meeting with the Old Ones. She had ordered the Fae to stockpile fruits and vegetables and cultivate the land as best they could, but they needed to know more. King Farrion reached around her to ruffle the deep magenta hair of his eldest daughter, the heir to the throne, Princess Vidya.

Vidya turned her green eyes upward in surprise, and when she saw who it was, a bright smile spread across her face. Her pink and gold wings fluttered with excitement.

"Father!" she whispered, reaching to hug him.

"Hello, my love," said the King as he put his arms around her.

"I'm glad you're back!"

The Eucalyptus leaves sticking out from the front pocket of his jacket tickled her cheek, and she sneezed. She released him quickly as he patted her on the back. Vidya looked from her father's eucalyptus branch to the pink rose sticking out of her mother's pocket and back to her own empty hands. She sighed and clenched her fists. Fae children were supposed to discover their guardian plant by their seventh birthday, but here she was at ten and still no plant had spoken to her in the way a guardian plant should. Her teachers had shown her hundreds of plants, but she felt nothing. There wasn't anything she could do except to wait and hope, and that worried her greatly.

A rolling movement from the large pocket at the front of her dress distracted her. She grinned and patted the pocket as a tiny claw reached up and out, gripping the edge of the fabric, quickly followed by a tiny, round, furry face.

"Good morning, Pancake," she whispered, reaching into the pocket and pulling the small, furry, round creature out. Pancake was a Quokka, a rare creature found only on a small island off Australia's western coast. The Fae had saved him from criminals a few months ago. They had been smuggling rare creatures when her father caught them and rescued him. When Vidya had first seen him, he had been hiding at the bottom of his cage, trying hard not to be seen, flattening himself right at the bottom, just like a pancake. And so that had become his name. They had been fast friends ever since, so much so that as well as the long slits in her dress that all Fae had to let their wings out, Vidya had made the palace seamstress sew large pockets on all her dresses so that Pancake had a space to feel safe. When he wasn't in her pocket, Pancake travelled around on Vidya's shoulder, gripping onto her ear for support. That's where he went now, climbing up onto her left shoulder and holding on tight, peering around at everyone with his little black eyes. Everyone loved Pancake with his little round ears, belly, and long tail, and most people kept a berry or two in their pockets just for him.

A whisper to her left caught her attention. Vidya looked around in the dim blue light and saw the confused face of little Daisy, her cousin. She caught the younger girl's eye, and Daisy grimaced sleepily back, pulling at the sparkling net that kept her purple curls off her face. Her wings twitched tiredly.

"Vidya," Daisy whispered, coming to stand next to her. "Can you remind me why we're standing here at the crack of dawn? Mother told me to shush."

Vidya smiled and bent a little to whisper into the little girl's ear, one hand on Pancake's round tummy, making sure he didn't fall off. The quokka leaned in to kiss Daisy on the cheek, making her giggle.

"Every year, the Fae gather on the first dawn of spring. We bring our guardian plants with us because when the sun rises above the forest, it's a magical dawn. Our guardian plants will light up and show us the power of nature. The power that's in all of us. The plants will give us food, and we'll go and eat in a grand feast. It's so exciting, you'll see!"

Daisy's green eyes grew wide with excitement. "There'll be a feast afterward?"

Vidya covered her mouth to smother a laugh. "Just you wait, Daisy, wait till you see the way the sun lights up the trees and the plants. It's so beautiful, it's like it fills the plants with all this power. And when the plants dance, we'll dance too."

The deep blue sky lightened with an orange glow, and the Fae playing the flutes and drums sped up the rhythm of their song. Adult Fae tucked the branches and cuttings of their guardian plants into pockets, and holding hands with one another, began a slow circular dance around the lawn. Gentle nudges pushed the children into the middle of the group, and Vidya tugged Daisy's hand into her own. Taking the hand of another Fae child with her other hand, the children began their own dance within the circle of adults, and soon, as the orange glow of dawn became brighter, they danced to the beat of the music in a magnificent whirl of colour.

The sun peeked over the treetops, and Vidya turned to grin at Daisy. She couldn't wait for her baby cousin to see how wonderful the dawn show was. Fae magic was so powerful, and it was beautiful when it was at its best, right at the start of spring. Her heart beat so fast with excitement in that moment, she didn't even care that she didn't have a guardian plant of her own, the way the plants would light up with magic would make up for it today.

The golden light of the sun spilled over the trees

and onto the palace behind them, and the musicians played faster still, and the dancing Fae twirled and spun, laughing and grinning now. Here it came, their smiles said, the magic of spring!

As Vidya twirled to the music, Pancake holding onto her ear for dear life, she searched the crowd for her parents. Her mother was patting baby Mahiya to the beat at the edge of the group, smiling at the rest of them dancing. But Vidya caught sight of her father's expression, and she missed her step, tripping a little. She quickly recovered and turned to look at him again. His face was serious, his mouth sat in a straight grim line, his powerful arms crossed firmly across his chest. Why did he look so worried? But his eyes were fixed on the crowd, as if they were searching for something. Waiting for something.

Vidya focused back on the dance, watching as the morning arrived and the sun's light shone upon them all, revealing the true colours of the hair and wings of the dancing Fae. She waited excitedly, heart thumping as the sun lit up the flowers, branches, and leaves of the plants of the Fae, and she held her own breath, waiting to exclaim and show Daisy the marvel of the show. Daisy looked around excitedly, cheeks flushed pink from dancing. But as the sun rose higher, they watched… but nothing happened.

Vidya looked into the faces of the adults dancing around them. They were looking at each other in confusion, looking up at the sun and back down at their guardian plants with furrowed brows.

They danced for a minute longer before the music

slowed down and the Fae slowed their steps, perplexed expressions on the previously excited faces.

"Did it happen?" asked Daisy, frowning, coming to a stop. "Was that it? Did I miss it?"

Vidya shook her head as the Fae adults moved from foot to foot and began speaking in low voices. Pancake's little head whipped around, trying to see everything at once.

"What's happening?" she heard someone behind her say.

"Why didn't the plants light up like they normally do?" said another.

"Did we get the day wrong?" a child squeaked.

Daisy tugged at the green sleeve of Vidya's dress. "Vidya, what happened? I don't get it."

But just as Vidya opened her mouth to tell her she had no clue, vivid blue wings fluttered next to her ear, and she almost groaned. She knew who it was before she turned.

Standing there with wide eyes were her annoying triplet cousins. At the same age at her, Lobey, Luna, and Toad were identical triplets with straight electric blue hair and wings. Those weren't their proper names, of course, but it was what Vidya had been calling them for years.

"What's happening?" asked Linaria, known as Toad because her guardian plant was the Toadflax plant.

Lunaria, or Luna, rubbed her arms anxiously. "That wasn't supposed to happen, was it?"

"Of course not," said Lobelia, or Lobey, crossly, a

deep frown on her face. "As heir to the throne, Vidya knows that this is not a good sign."

Vidya tried very hard not to roll her eyes at Lobey, the eldest triplet and forever her rival. The only thing that made them even was that Lobey didn't know her guardian plant either.

"Why isn't it a good sign?" piped Daisy, purple wings twitching anxiously.

Lobey gave her a superior look and looked down her nose at Daisy. "Because, cousin, the spring light shows the power of Fae magic in all its glory. The fact that the magic didn't happen is *very,* very bad."

The five cousins exchanged a look of worry as the whispering around them grew.

"I'm going to speak to my parents," said Vidya, pushing past Toad to get to the edge of the group.

But as she got to the edge of the garden, she found both her parents stepping onto the wooden dais they used to stand upon to give speeches.

Her father raised his hands, and everyone shushed. A hundred pairs of green eyes turned to watch the King and Queen. The Queen gently patted baby Mahiya and beckoned Vidya to come and stand next to them. Vidya padded forward and stood next to her mother on the dais. Wings twitched in uncertainty all around her as she stared into the worried faces of the Fae.

"Something is happening," boomed King Farrion in a loud, serious voice. As Vidya looked at his even face, she noticed no surprise, only determination.

He knew, Vidya realised. *He's not surprised at all—he*

knew this was going to happen. What did the Old Ones tell him?

"The Fae magic has… changed somehow," he continued. "There is nothing to be alarmed about at this stage. The Queen and I will call a council to figure out our next steps."

The surrounding Fae exchanged looks of fear. Wings twitched and brows furrowed.

"Everyone needs to go about their day as normal," the Queen said in a calm voice that carried across the lawn. "We will let you know when things become clear to us. We are sure it will all be sorted out quickly."

The Fae magic has changed. Fae were whispering to each other. What did that mean? Lobey had said that it had 'failed'. Was that really what had happened? Nothing like this had ever happened before in the history of the Fae, as Vidya knew it from what her teachers had told her. Fae magic was as sure as nature itself. But there was one big problem Vidya could see as she looked back up to the stern face of her father. The Fae were made of Fae magic. If it was failing. What on earth did that mean for them?

2

TROUBLE COMES IN THREES

All things are One. The Fae are one with the soil, the plants, the trees. The Fae are one with the animals. To be Fae means to look into the eyes of another and know they are one part of the same whole.

—The Book of the Fae, Queen Mab the First, 3333 B.C.

There was no breakfast feast that year for the Eastern Bushland Fae. Instead, everyone shuffled off back to an ordinary day's work, shrugging at each other. 'Don't panic,' the King had said, and so, the Fae, being trusting people with good faith in a King who had never failed to protect them and a Queen who ran the city wisely, went about their day as normal, the worry cast back to the furthest corners of their minds.

But Princess Vidya was thinking.

The children were rounded up and taken to their

classes, which for the ten-year-olds meant gathering in the palace library with Master Sunny, a yellow-haired Fae so elderly that his wings were almost completely see-through. Vidya had never seen him fly, and so she wasn't even sure his wings could work at all. The Fae were nothing if not polite people, and it was considered bad manners to flap your wings around if you could walk instead, but in 'flying areas' such as out in the city, everyone chose to fly.

Princess Vidya, Pancake, the blue triplets, and ten other Fae children the same age sat at rectangular wooden tables in front of a blackboard, upon which Master Sunny was drawing a detailed diagram of a small goblin sized man in red and white chalk. They had tried to get him to talk about what had happened that morning, but the old teacher shrugged and directed them back to the King's words to 'not worry'. So, they continued in their classes on the creatures of the Fae forest.

"Yara-ma-yha-who are dangerous creatures on their own," he said in his ancient, dry voice. "What makes them even more fearsome is that they always work in a tribe."

Pancake was on his belly on the table Vidya sat at, a pen and paper in front of him, copying the picture of the creature in slow, careful strokes. Vidya had to admit that he was getting quite good at drawing. She squinted at the diagram of the small red goblin on the blackboard. His head was bigger than his body, and on his hands and feet, Master Sunny had drawn small round circles.

"Excuse me, Master Sunny," Vidya called. "What are those on his hands?"

A little way down the table, she heard Lobey made a rude snorting noise. Vidya ignored her as Master Sunny turned, stroking his long, faded, yellow beard.

"Ah," he said. "Those are the most concerning things of all." He lifted his own hands, wiggling his fingers. "Yarama have suckers on their hands and feet. They use these for several things. Climbing trees, and—" he lowered his voice as if revealing a great secret, and the class leaned in to hear, "—they use them to take your nose right off."

The class exclaimed loudly, Pancake made a retching noise.

"Didn't you already know that?" sneered Lobey to the others. "Aunty Sandy had her nose stolen last year."

"Ah, yes," wheezed Master Sunny. "If I remember correctly, the Duchess luckily had her nose put right back in place by the King the next day."

He pointed a stern finger at them. "Stories like these warn us of the perils of the Fae forest. It is with good reason Fae are not allowed beyond the boundary set by Queen Mab the second thousands of years ago."

"But how did Uncle Farrion get her nose back?" asked Luna, anxiously pulling on a blue lock of hair.

"*King* Farrion," Lobey corrected as Luna rolled her eyes.

"Well," said Master Sunny, "being the ruler of the Fae comes with many perks. The ruling King or Queen can talk to *all* plants. Not just their guardian plant. Secondly, upon their coronation, they can create a new plant all together, thus the creation of the Book Tree, the Messenger Tree, and many of the Portal Trees. But the most important thing of all is that all creatures of the Fae forest are bound by the King's Law. And that means, in the Safe Zone, there is a truce, and no creature may harm a Fae in that part of the forest. That is the rule created by the old Fae. It has never been broken."

A yell sounded from outside the library, followed by several loud shouting voices. Toad twitched violently, and Vidya and Lobey jumped out of their seats, Pancake leapt from the table into Vidya's arms, burying his nose in the crook of her elbow.

"Remain where you are!" roared Master Sunny, rushing toward the library entrance. The stern look he gave them made Vidya and Lobey freeze on the spot. "I will see what it is."

Vidya stepped from foot to foot, her magenta wings dancing, itching to follow. But Master Sunny had taught her since she was a baby, and she knew he was almost always right. She patted Pancake reassuringly and exchanged a worried glance with Lobey, Toad, and Luna. Vidya strained her ears to listen to what was going on outside. The library was right next to the main entrance to the palace, so whatever was happening there had probably come from outside. There were a few loud voices talking at once, but not loud enough to make out the words. She heard Master Sunny's deep commanding voice and the other voices went quiet. There were shuffling sounds. It was all too much for Vidya. She needed to know what was happening.

"I'm not waiting," muttered Vidya, pushing her chair aside. "I'm going to see what it is."

Vidya, cradling the still trembling Pancake, strode across the library toward the large double entrance doors, but just as she put her hand on the handle to open it, the door swung open, and Master Sunny, pale faced with his yellow hair askew, rushed through. Pancake jumped in her arms, and Master Sunny frowned deeply upon seeing them standing there.

"I believe I told you to remain where you were, Princess," he said disapprovingly.

"What happened?" Vidya asked, nervously.

Master Sunny quickly closed the door behind him, making sure that Vidya couldn't see anything in the entrance hall. "It remains to be seen," he said in a dark voice.

Vidya made a face. That was not an answer at all, but Master Sunny was striding quickly back toward the class, and Vidya had no choice but to follow him.

"What's going on?" Lobey asked in a voice that was even more rude than usual. Vidya returned to her seat, pulling Pancake into her lap.

The old Master came to stand in front of the class, a look of deep thought on his face. For a long moment, he didn't answer, and the students held their breaths.

"Nothing is certain at the moment," he finally said, his voice tight. "But I'm sure it will reveal itself with time."

"What does that mean?" sneered Lobey, unimpressed. "It sounded like someone was hurt or something bad—"

Master Sunny held up his hand and gave Lobey a stern look. She felt silent immediately but had to chew on her own lip to control herself.

"The Fae are resilient people, Lobey, remember that. When winter comes, we weather the storms and wait until spring comes again. Why is that? What makes the Fae brave?"

It was Willow, a navy haired, quiet boy whose guardian plant was the Bilberry and was the strongest aim with a bow Vidya had ever seen, who answered in a soft voice that was barely heard. "Because we know that spring will always come."

Master Sunny stared at navy haired boy for a moment and then nodded slowly. "That's right, Willow. Like the passing of the seasons, the good always follows the bad."

Vidya turned to see Lobey giving Master Sunny an unimpressed look, her face screwed up in annoyance.

That's two strange things that's happened today, Vidya thought. *What are the adults trying to hide from us?*

Vidya and Pancake watched Master Sunny carefully. His eyes were fixed upon the blackboard, but Vidya had the feeling he wasn't looking at his diagram on there at all. He looked as if he were seeing something very far away. He mouthed something to himself and fingered the edge of his long black robe. Then he shook his head once, scratched his ear, and nodded. Vidya had seen that look on adults' faces before. It was the face of an adult trying to decide if they should reveal something important.

"There is an old story I would like to tell you," he said. He fidgeted with the edge of his sleeve this time. Vidya thought he looked quite suddenly exhausted.

"Willow," he called. "Find me a book about the creature called, 'the Bunyip'."

Willow shot out of his chair and walked over to the large table set in the corner of the library. On it sat an ancient miniature tree called a Bonsai. Except this tree was different to other Bonsai because of the long vines attached to his sides. In front of the tree on the table sat a wide box filled with tiny green cards made of square leaves.

"Book Tree!" Willow called in a loud voice. You always had to make sure to speak loudly to the Book Tree, as his hearing had gotten worse in his old age. "I need a book about the Bunyip." The little Bonsai lifted a vine-arm up. The little fingers on the end of the vine were lifted against his trunk in the way that people did when they didn't hear what you said.

"BUNYIP!" Willow practically shouted.

The Book Tree shook its topmost leaves as if nodding in understanding. His vine-arms shot out in front of him, fingers hovering over the box of leaf-cards, thinking. After a second, he reached into the box and plucked out two cards, holding them out to Willow.

The navy haired boy accepted the cards and read them out loud.

"'The Bunyip: Sightings and Stories' and 'Indigenous

Legends'." He looked up at Master Sunny, listening keenly by his blackboard.

"The first one, Willow, if you please."

Willow nodded and returned the cards back to the Book Tree, who took it back and placed it in its original spot within the box in front of him. Willow trotted away from the class into the many rows of bookshelves on the other side of the library. Vidya could see him scanning the shelves, and after a minute he slipped out a small book and brought it back to the class, handing it over to Master Sunny.

"Let's see," he wheezed, leafing through the pages. "Here we go. I can't quite draw this one as well." He held up the open book for them to all to see a painting of a large black creature that looked like a cross between a gigantic black dog and a seal.

From Vidya's lap, Pancake sat up with interest, then squeaked with disgust.

"Urgh," said Toad, flicking her electric blue hair. "Is that a Bunyip?"

"Indeed. They are creatures of the human realm," said Master Sunny, turning the book over to read from it.

"Of the most fearsome of mythical creatures in Australia is the Bunyip. With the body of a large seal and the head of a most gruesome dog, the Bunyip swims and runs with equal strength, patrolling the length of the Murray River, his terrifying call can be heard for miles. Stroll down the Murray river after dark, and be sure that if a Bunyip sets his sights on you, there is no return."

Master Sunny snapped the book shut and looked out at them all with a stern eye.

"This book was written in 1780. Shortly after, the rates of Bunyip attacks in the human realm increased tenfold. The humans were so terrified, in the end, King Fern, Vidya's grandfather, being the Fae King and guardian of both plants and animals, intervened. He enlisted the help of Queen Talia, the Mermaid Queen of the Western Pacific Ocean, to help."

"What did they do?" asked Toad in a hushed voice, "they didn't hunt them, did they?"

"Well, as you know, the first rule of the Fae is *'do no harm unto another living being'*. But the Bunyips were not creatures that were open to conversation, they only think of their next dinner. There is nothing else on their minds. So, King Fern devised a grand plan. With the help of the merpeople, to cut the Bunyips off from escaping through the river, the Fae rounded up the Bunyips one by one and brought them here, into the Fae realm, into the secret cave system deep in the Fae forest."

"But how did they get them into the Fae realm?" asked Vidya, imagining that rounding up scary creatures and bringing them all the way here would have been no simple task.

"The Fae pond system," said Master Sunny, leaning back on his desk with a faint smile on his face. "Brilliant, really. The Fae ponds are small pools that exist all over the Fae realm, and they lead right into secret locations in the ocean. This is the way the Fae people and the merpeople under the ocean have spoken to each other for thousands of years."

Vidya leaned back in her chair and shook her head. If she was to be queen one day, and take over her father's job, she would have to be just as clever to come up with answers to problems just like this one. She listened keenly as Master Sunny continued.

"King Fern sealed the Bunyips in this cave. But the cleverest thing was this. In the centre of the cave was a pool of water. Not a Fae pond, mind you, a magic pool full of extra strong Jilungin dreaming potion."

The name of the herb rang a bell in Vidya's mind. Jilungin was one of the plants the Masters had tried to test her with not that long ago. It was a plant that made you go to sleep.

"So, in that cave, all alone with no food or water, the Bunyips had no choice but to drink that Jilungin dreaming potion. And so, they fell into a timeless sleep, unable to hurt another human."

Master Sunny paused and gazed out the window, fidgeting again with the corner of his robe. He chewed on his lip as if thinking about something troubling.

"But nothing lasts forever…" he murmured.

Vidya's pink eyebrows shot up in surprise. Had she heard him right?

"What was that you just said, Master Sunny?"

The elderly Fae shook himself, as if trying to get rid of a bad thought. His wings twitched as he turned and, realising that his students were all staring at him, waved a hand at them.

"Nothing, nothing. There is no problem that our King and Queen cannot solve."

Just as Vidya was wondering if anyone else had caught Master Sunny's murmured words, she turned to see Lobey watching her with raised blue eyebrows. Vidya shrugged her shoulders at the girl as if to say, *'the grownups will take care of it'*.

3
THE DEVIL'S FINGERS

"The Fae are the Guardians of the forest. Each Fae guards their own flora. Like old friends, they speak without words, they love without agenda and they grow without judgement."

—The Book of the Fae, Queen Mab the First, 3333 B.C.

There was a rapid knock on the library door. The students all turned to look as one.

"Princess Vidya?" it was Sage, one of her father's assistants, peeking around the door, a tired Fae with crisp, light blue wings. "May I speak with the Princess?"

Vidya glanced at Master Sunny, who nodded, and she got out of her chair, placing Pancake into her pocket, and made her way to the door. Sage held out a folded and sealed piece of paper.

"His Majesty the King asks that you take this to the Dowager Queen Subbhya—your Nani," he rubbed his arms uncomfortably. "She is… with her trees in the last Greenhouse."

Realisation washed over Vidya, and she nodded her head in understanding. "Oh right, of course."

Her Nani, her mother's mother, was guardian of the most dangerous trees known to the Fae. The *Devil's Fingers* were carnivorous trees, which, in their case, meant that they liked to eat people. They had that name because the aggressive trees had gnarly hands with which they would reach out and grab passers-by. Once they had their victim, they would snatch them away into their trunk through an opening in the base where rows and rows of sharp teeth were ready and waiting to gobble them up.

The Fae married each other from all over the world to teach each other the way of different plants. Vidya's Nani had come from India to marry the Fae King of Tonga. Then, Vidya's mother, Queen Salote, had come from Tonga to Australia to marry King Farrion.

Once they were married, the King realised that his mother-in-law was the only Fae known to be the guardian of the Devil's Fingers. Because there were so many in the Fae forest here, King Farrion asked her if she would take responsibility of rounding them all up from the forest and keeping them in a triple locked greenhouse at the back of the palace. She agreed, of course, as it would mean she would get to be close to her daughter.

No one was permitted near the triple locked greenhouse where her Nani looked after the Devil's Fingers, it was far too dangerous. However, over the years, the strange plants had taken a liking to Vidya, and although they were not her Guardian plant, it meant she was one of the few people who could get to her Nani if she was working in there.

Vidya left the library and headed out to the back of the palace into the bright sunlight, walking down the path that led to the greenhouses. A light breeze tickled her cheek as she walked, and Pancake, having recovered from his earlier fright, climbed his way back up to her shoulder to enjoy the sun. Her mother's pink rose bushes lined the way and made the air smell sweet, and for the thousandth time, Vidya wondered when she would find her guardian plant.

"Darkness…" came a wispy voice.

Vidya whirled around to see a small echidna hobbling along on his hind legs, using a white cane for balance.

"Oh, Uncle Jula-wil it's you," said Vidya, relieved, crouching down so she was eye to eye with the elderly marsupial. She was eye to eye only in a manner of speaking, because Uncle Jula-wil, her father's oldest advisor, had two tiny black eye patches covering his eyes due to the fact that he was blind. No one actually knew how he got around the palace, or how he didn't fall off the edge into the Bottomless Sky for that matter, but when he was not in meetings with the King,

Uncle Jula-wil hobbled around the palace grounds, mumbling to himself.

"Princess," wheezed Uncle Jula-wil. "It approaches…"

"What do you mean, Uncle?" Vidya asked uncertainly, looking around to see if anyone else had noticed the elderly marsupial, but they were alone on the path.

Uncle Jula-wil tapped the white walking stick impatiently in front of him. "I can feel it in my spines, Princess," he wheezed. "Change is afoot. Darkness is afoot…"

Pancake squeaked disapprovingly in Vidya's ear.

"Weird!" cried Uncle Jula-wil waving his stick at Pancake. "What's weird is a grown quokka riding on the shoulder of a young Fae girl!"

Vidya turned her head to look at Pancake, alarmed.

"Be warned, Princess," muttered Uncle Julia-wil in a much quieter voice. "Darkness approaches. A choice must be made."

The little echidna abruptly turned to the left and began walking into the bushes, muttering quietly to himself. Vidya straightened from her crouch and watched him go, her magenta brows furrowed. She shook her head as his long black spines disappeared into the rose hedges. Her father had always insisted that the elderly echidna was not crazy, but when he started saying things like that, how could she *not* think he was nuts?

But… said a voice at the back of her mind, *think about what happened this morning.* First the Spring ritual, then the commotion in the palace during class. And now she held in her hand a special message for her Nani. The adults knew something was going on. Something big. Uncle Jula-wil was trying to tell her something in his own strange way.

Vidya tugged on a magenta curl as she began walking down the path again. Nani was always honest with her. *She* would tell her what was going on.

Sunlight glinted off the glass roofs of the greenhouses. Vidya walked down the rows and rows of them. Most held rare or dangerous plants, and their Fae guardians walked in and out, tending to their needs or harvesting from them for the Fae to eat or use in magical potions. One held the Ghostberry bushes, which made the Fae hard to see when they went out into the human realm. Another held tea tree plants which healed cuts, wounds, and insect bites.

The Devil's Fingers were kept in the last greenhouse, furthest away from the palace, behind an iron gate.

Vidya walked through the gate up to the solid glass doors of the greenhouse. Squinting to see if her grandmother was close by, she rang the metal bell to the side of the door.

No one was permitted inside without her Nani by their side. Otherwise, you were just asking to be eaten.

"Coming!" came her Nani's faint voice. Vidya could see her blurry form hurrying up to the entrance from the other side. Pancake tittered in protest on her shoulder, trying to climb down. Vidya grabbed him and put him in her pocket, safe and sound. He squeaked in fear, grasping the edges of the fabric, peering out over the top of his tiny claws.

The three locks on the door clanked one by one, and Vidya grinned, feeling so proud that her own Nani was the only one who could handle these dangerous plants. Her heart pounded as the door swung open, but Vidya knew she was safe with her Nani by her side.

"Oh, lovely girl!" Nani cooed when the door opened. Vidya was swept up in a warm hug. Nani smelled like soil and cinnamon at the same time. She had deep-red wings and hair that reminded Vidya of the colour of a ladybug's shell, and she wore lipstick in a matching colour.

"Hi, Nani," said Vidya as she was released. "I have a message for you from father."

Nani glanced at the green paper in her hand and frowned before looking back up to peer at her, brown face concerned, then nodded.

"Hmm," she said. "There is worry in your face, child. Come in and let us see what we can do about it."

Vidya followed her into the darkness of the greenhouse. The air was warm and sticky in here, just how the Devil's Fingers liked it, just like their native home in the deepest darkest parts of the Fae forest. Nani took Vidya's hand and held up a bright lantern in the other to lead the two of them through the middle of the greenhouse. The dark branches of the Devil's Fingers swayed threateningly over them. Vidya squinted at them, eyeing the thick brown leathery trunks and watching nervously for signs of sudden movement. She took a deep breath and smelled the sweet perfume they emitted to lure in their prey. It smelled just like sweet mangoes, and she shivered at how easy it would be to fool someone who didn't know about that trick of theirs.

Nani bore no signs of nervousness, however. She stomped through the path, chin held high, staring down at the dark trees on either side of her.

Suddenly, a barky hand lurched out of the shadows, headed straight for Vidya. She gasped and lurched backward, but quick as a frog snapping up a fly, Nani whirled around and gave the Devils' Fingers a sharp slap with her hand.

"Oi, you!" she shouted.

The dark hand fell under her slap and quivered as if ashamed of itself and retreated slowly backward into the darkness of its tree.

"That is very rude," said Nani loudly. "If I see anybody else and *I mean anybody*—" She whirled around to the front this time and pointed to trees on the other side of the path. "—trying anything with *my granddaughter*, you'll be *very* sorry."

Even Vidya shrank back, hearing her angry words. Nani sure had a way of putting people in line.

"Humph!"

Nani grabbed Vidya's hand more tightly and began striding down the path again, a little faster this time.

On the other side of the greenhouse was another glass door leading to a large bedroom, complete with a comfy couch. The wall here was also glass, so Nani could watch her trees as she slept. Vidya sat down on the couch and watched her grandmother pour them two glasses of chilled Ghostberry juice. This was the main juice the Fae drank. It was poisonous to humans, but for the Fae, the sweet liquid made sure the humans would not see them when they ventured out into the human realm. To humans, the Fae would look like parts of the forest, they wouldn't be able to see them at all.

Nani sat down on the couch, mopping her forehead with a pink cloth. Vidya didn't know how she stayed in this damp heat all day and all night, Vidya was already sticky with sweat. She gulped down her juice gratefully.

"You'll never guess what's happening, Nani," Vidya said, setting her glass down on the side table and passing over the letter. "I didn't see you at the spring ritual this morning."

Nani opened the letter. "No," she said, "I needed to be here."

Vidya watched her Nani anxiously as the older lady's eyes moved back and forth across the page. In moments, she re-folded the paper and placed it on the side table, sighing. She rubbed her eyes and cast her gaze out the window where the Devil's Fingers were swaying.

"What is it, Nani?" said Vidya in a quiet voice.

"It is worse than I thought," Nani said. "I heard about the Dawn Ritual, Vidya, and I thought that was bad enough, but now this…" she waved to the letter on the table.

"We heard a commotion this morning during class," said Vidya, sitting forward in her chair. "But Master Sunny would not tell us what it was."

"He did not want to scare the children," said Nani, rubbing her eyes tiredly. "But as Princess, I think you should know. There is a very real risk we are facing here." Nani leaned forward and looked at Vidya. "There was an attack in the Fae forest today. In the Safe Zone."

Vidya sat bolt upright. "But that's impossible!"

Nani nodded. "It should be impossible, yes. The King's word is Law, and his word was that no creature of the forest within the boundary can harm a Fae. But… this very thing happened. Captain Silver and her patrol were attacked by an unknown beast."

Vidya's heart pounded in her chest. Her mind raced, trying to make sense of this new information and trying to add it all up. These things happening together could not be a coincidence.

"I also have news for your father." Nani continued. "I don't want to scare you, Vidya, but as crown Princess, I think you should know the truth. I can feel it in the air. In the trees…."

She paused and sipped from her glass. Vidya could not help but stare at her Nani. How could things get any worse?

Nani pointed through the glass to the nearest tree. Vidya could just see it by the dim light of the lantern. It was a sapling—a young tree with thin branches still growing in a pot. The gnarled branches on this tree were still, they were not swaying at all. In fact, they drooped downward and made the little thing look rather sad. Tiny spindly hands rested on either side of it. No, Vidya saw, no hands at all, just one hand. It only had the one.

"My saplings are dying," said Nani.

Vidya's head whipped to stare at her. *Dying* was not a word the Fae knew. Plants, trees, and flowers *did not die* under their care. The magic that kept them alive was too strong, and they were good guardians of their trees. They knew them in and out, and plants *thrived* with the Fae.

"I've tried everything, my love," continued Nani. "But the saplings just won't grow. They get tired and droop, they stop growing and eventually…."

She did not have to finish her sentence because Vidya could see for herself. She had seen plants die in the human realm.

Nani took a deep breath and looked sternly at Vidya. "It is not only my trees, Vidya. I have seen it happening to the other plants in the royal greenhouses."

Ice trickled down Vidya's chest, and she stared at her grandmother in disbelief.

"How?" asked Vidya, horrified. "Why?"

"The Fae magic is faltering, Vidya," said Nani, sighing. "I cannot imagine why, or how. Or even how we can fix it. But that is the truth. Fae magic…. it's trembling and failing. And I think… Somehow, this beast in the forest is connected to our situation. It cannot be a coincidence."

Vidya's mind raced. The beast in the forest was interfering with their magic somehow? What on Earth could it be? Nothing was strong enough to do that. Nothing! The Fae had been here since the earth was new, since the land emerged from the sea, and nothing in that time had ever threatened their magic before. What on earth could it be?

"Your mother is busy with baby Mahiya," continued Nani. "We will have to pull our weight and work together."

Vidya agreed, baby Mahi was only a new baby, and with sparks flying from her every other second, she needed great care to look after. Her mother would be busy for quite some time.

"I can help," said Vidya. "I can research in the library, see if there's anything there."

Nani smiled warmly and patted her shoulder.

"That's a good place to start. You were always my clever girl," she said, getting to her feet. "Now, I have some work to do of my own. Your father will not have wanted me to tell you all this, Vidya. He might think you are too young. But the thing is, Fae magic is strongest in our children. If it is fading, the children will be the ones we look to for magic. I think it's good that you know."

Vidya nodded. She had a lot to think about.

They stood and made their way back toward the entrance of the greenhouse with Vidya's hand clasped firmly in Nani's.

"Are they telling you anything?" asked Vidya. "Are the Devil's Fingers telling you anything about the Fae magic changing?"

The older lady kept her eyes moving between the deadly trees on either side of the path but nodded.

"They feel something, alright. The dark trees can feel it more than the others. They know something is there, but far away and faint. They just can't tell me anything specific. If I'm honest, I feel a bit off too. Like something is weighing me down, making me tired."

Vidya sighed, thinking about how useful having a guardian plant would be right now. "I hope I find my guardian plant soon. I'd even be happy if it was the skunk flower right now!"

They reached the entrance, and Nani took her key out again, undoing all three locks. As she opened the door, light spilled through, and Vidya squinted at the sudden brightness. When her eyes adjusted, her grandmother reached forward and hugged her tightly.

"I remember thinking the exact same thing—" she leaned back and tugged Vidya's chin lightly, "—with the exact same sad face. I found my guardian when I was twelve. It's late, to be sure, but it was only because my old friends are rare and dangerous trees. So it stands to reason, that when you find yours, it will be a plant you never expected. Something rare and wonderful. Little known to most people. There are some wonderful plants out here, Vidya. I just know when you find out what it is, it will be well worth the wait."

4

THE KING'S WARNING

The Fae poets will write sonnets of the way the wind moves through the trees. The way sunlight kisses the petals of a flower. But the thing they will write most about is the way the Fae tend to their guardian plant. A love like that does not exist anywhere else.

—The Book of the Fae, Queen Mab the First, 3333 B.C.

Vidya woke up with a start and realised she had been drooling on top of an old book called 'The Legend of the Flower of Awakening'.

"Yuck," she said, wiping the pages of the book with the sleeve of her dress.

She had been researching about Fae magic late last night, and this book told the story that all Fae parents told their children at bed-time. That, at the dawn of time, the Flower of Awakening sung her song and woke the Fae up from the earth. The Fae then sprung onto the land and learned the song of the flower and came to know themselves. The flower gave them knowledge and wisdom, instructing them they were to be guardians of the earth forevermore. But it was just a bedtime story. A fairytale. A myth.

A noise like the whistle of a bird drew Vidya's attention to the corner of the room. She was surprised to see Master Sunny snoring, sitting slumped in his teacher's chair, his chin resting on his chest, rising and falling with each snore.

Vidya looked out the window. The sun was high in the sky. She sat up straight in alarm. She had come into the library after dinner to do some research like Nani had told her to do. Had she actually slept here *all* night? Why had nobody woken her up and told her to go to bed?

She stretched and looked around the library, and her eyes fell upon a librarian stretched out on her tummy on the floor, purple wings folded around her, sleeping with her head resting on an arm. She recognised her as Librarian Rose, a cranky old Fae who didn't like her books touched. That was unusual. Why would Rose be sleeping on the floor? Vidya quickly stood and rushed over to the old Fae to see if she was okay, casting her eye about to see if anyone else in the library had noticed. But there was no one else in the library at all. When she reached Rose, she touched her arm.

"Hello, Rose? Are you alright?" she asked.

The librarian made no move, just continued to snore. Vidya stood up.

Had someone tricked the librarians into taking a sleeping potion? That would make a funny joke to be sure, but she just couldn't imagine anyone doing that. A joke isn't very funny when the people you're playing the joke on are too fast asleep to laugh about it.

Looking around and seeing nobody else, Vidya walked toward Master Sunny.

"Master Sunny, are you alright?" she asked in a loud voice. She poked him, but he made no response. She jumped back in surprise. What was going on?

The door behind her flew open with a *BANG*, and a blur of electric blue wings rushed toward her.

"Help!" Toad cried as the triplets screeched to a halt in front of her.

"Oh my Earth, Vidya!" cried Luna.

"We have a seriously big problem," said Lobey in a disgusted voice.

"What's going on?" Vidya asked, looking at each of them in turn. Outside, she could hear a couple of kids calling out to each other.

"It's the adults," said Lobey, walking over to Master Sunny, poking him hard on the forehead. "See? They're all dead asleep. Won't wake up."

"We tried throwing water on them," wailed Toad. "And then we tried pinching them, but nothing is working!"

Vidya's mind raced. *Her parents*. She pushed

through Lobey and Luna and ran as fast as she could out of the library, using her wings to move her faster along. She got to the stairs that led to higher levels and shot upward straight into the air, propelling herself into the King and Queen's rooms.

"Mother!" she cried, racing into her parent's room. Vidya pushed open the door and found her mother and baby Mahiya snuggled up on her parents' bed. She walked up to them, feeling the triplets enter the room behind her. Her mother slept peacefully, as did baby Mahiya, who grumbled, turned, and opened her mouth, suckling at her mother's breast.

"Mahiya is awake, it looks like," she breathed.

A groan made all four of them look to the far side of the room. Vidya frowned and rushed to the other side of the bed where she found her father lying on the floor. He looked like he had fallen out of the bed.

"Father!" she cried, rushing over to crouch next to him.

"Vidya…." her father mumbled with his eyes still closed. "Vidya…"

"What's going on, father?" she asked quickly. "What do I do?"

"Fae magic is fading," he tried to lift his head, but failed and weakly lay back down. "Stronger… in children… prepare, Vidya… keep… safe."

"Prepare for what?"

The king coughed, fighting the sleep. He choked out a single word.

"War."

Vidya's heart turned to ice as her father's head fell

back and he began snoring just like Master Sunny. She looked up to meet Lobey's eyes, shining with fear.

"He said—"

"I heard what he said, Lobey," said Vidya roughly, getting to her feet.

"War?" whispered Luna, "Did he really mean *war* war?"

"Don't know what other type of war there is, really," said Lobey dully.

Wings twitched anxiously as the girls stood staring down at the King in silence.

"But the Fae have never fought a… *war*." Toad spat the word like it was something gross she had found under her shoe. Vidya chewed on her lip and shook her head in agreement. The Fae had never needed to fight in any way against any sort of enemy. Ill-meaning humans sometimes, yes, but never in the Fae realm.

"But a war against what?" asked Toad softly. The triplets exchanged shrugs, blue wings jostling up and down.

"It's got to be something to do with what happened yesterday!" Lobey threw her hands in the air angrily. "When we were in class, remember? The commotion Master Sunny wouldn't let us know about! Something happened right then!"

"No," said Luna. "It can't—"

"Lobey is right," said Vidya, breathing in deeply. Three pairs of the forest green eyes spun to stare at her. *They should know*, she decided. *Everyone needed to know.*

"There was an attack," said Vidya. "Nani told me. It

was in the letter I was asked to take to her. Yesterday morning, Captain Silver and her patrol were attacked by something in the Safe Zone."

"That's impossible," whispered Toad.

Vidya nodded. "That's exactly what I said. But Nani seemed to think that with the Fae magic fading, something is changing."

"So you think whatever attacked Captain Silver is going to start a war with us?" asked Lobey with a deep frown. "I just can't imagine this happening, really, I can't—"

"Well, it is happening," said Vidya irritably, gesturing at her father snoring on the floor. "Look around us, Lobey. Everything is going wrong. My father wouldn't just say something if he didn't mean it. If he says we are to prepare for war, then that is what we will do."

Vidya's jaw was set, and she knew she was right. Her father had given her instructions, and so she would follow them. There wasn't really a choice she could see.

"But, Vidya," pleaded Luna, stepping forward, wings drooping. "The Fae have followed one rule since we woke up from the beginning of the earth."

"Do no harm unto another being," stressed Toad. "War means fighting. It means hurting something. And if it's true this thing in the forest is out to hurt us, we are not allowed to hurt it."

But Lobey stepped forward this time. "No," she said slowly. "We are Fae children. The exception to the first rule is us. Fae children are allowed to hurt other crea- tures if it means defending ourselves."

Vidya's magenta brows furrowed deeply at Lobey's words. It was true; she was right. Vidya had herself injured a human saving The Unicorn Princess Sonakshi just earlier this year. She had used her bow to shoot an arrow at the poacher, Glen, while he kept Princess Sonakshi under lock and key. All Fae children knew the rule.

"It's not right," said Luna, shaking her head.

"None of this is right," said Vidya. "You heard my father. The King has given us instructions."

That seemed to shake them out of their fear. The triplets nodded slowly. Whatever was happening, the King's word was Law, and they had to follow that.

"First thing," said Vidya. "We should check on all the parents," she said. "We can't have people sleeping in dangerous positions, like in a Fae pond, or half out of a tree. Let's make sure everyone is safe. After that, tell all the kids to meet in the entrance hall of the Palace. Tell them Princess Vidya is calling a meeting."

The triplets nodded.

"Everyone is probably frightened," said Luna. "What are you going to tell them at the meeting?"

Vidya chewed her lip. She had no idea, so she just waved her hand at them.

"First, I need to find Nani. I'm worried she's stuck in with the Devil's Fingers."

Luna gasped. "Oh god, what if they eat her?"

Vidya didn't want to think about that. "That's why we have to hurry. You three spread the word about finding the adults and the meeting. Toad, you're the best with babies, can you come back and look after baby Mahiya? I'll go to the greenhouse."

"I'll come with you," said Lobey bossily, to which Vidya frowned. "It's too dangerous," said Lobey. "At least two of us should go. Plus, I've always wanted to see them. Now's my chance."

Vidya shook her head and shrugged. Once Lobey got something into her head, she wouldn't let it go. There was no use arguing with her.

"Fine, you two," she waved at Luna and Toad. "Be bossy, tell everyone to meet us in the entrance hall in one hour. Got it?"

They nodded, and, blue braids swinging, ran out of the room.

Lobey and Vidya followed, making their way out of the palace and into the garden.

"I need to send a letter first," said Vidya, veering off to the left where the Messenger Tree sat. A short, fat gum tree created by one of the old Queens so they could communicate easily with other people far away.

Vidya clasped her hands in front of the tree. "Messenger Tree, I need a leaf to send a letter, please." A second later, a broad leaf fluttered down from high in the branches. Vidya grabbed the leaf from the ground and taking a pen out of her pocket, roughly scribbled a message on it.

She threw it into the air with a jump. Whispering the name of the person she wanted it to go to. With a magical wind, the leaf whipped into the air.

"Who are you sending that message to?" asked Lobey suspiciously.

Vidya watched the leaf as it spun high into the air away from them. "A good friend from the Blue Mountains I haven't seen in a while," she said softly. "The Unicorn Princess, Sonakshi of Macuata."

Lobey looked impressed. "Will she help us?"

"I helped her once, and she has her own unicorn magic. And right now, we need all we can get."

Lobey nodded, and they continued down the greenhouse path, all the way down to the end.

When they reached the door to the forbidden greenhouse, Vidya chewed her lip. It was locked from the inside. How would they get in? An inkling feeling in her chest made her reach up and knock firmly on the door three times. "It's me!" she called in to the glass. "Princess Vidya looking for my Nani!" She held her breath and waited.

The three locks of the thick glass door opened one by one. *Clunk. Clunk. Clunk.*

Lobey and Vidya exchanged a worried look. If Nani was asleep, who was opening the door? Without a word, the two girls took three steps back from the door and waited.

The greenhouse door slowly swung outwards with a long *creaaaaaaaak* and a brown branch snaked out, pushing the door wide open. A menacing dark tree stomped through the doorway, using its roots as feet, its long arm-like branches planted themselves on its trunk, looking like an angry old man with his hands on his hips.

Vidya and Lobey glanced at each other, and before Vidya could do anything, Lobey stomped forward and met the Devil's Finger front on.

"Listen, you!" shouted Lobey, her own hands on her hips. "No mean tricks, or funny business. We're here on a mission, and Nani might be hurt. We're here to see if she's okay, and you're gonna let us do that. Got it?"

The tree, the size of an enormous man, remained stock still for a moment. Lobey glared at the tree and the tree glared back, but Lobey did not back down. Vidya felt the strange urge to laugh as the girl and the terrifying tree stared at each other. But quite quickly, the arms of the tree fell to its side, and he turned, using a barky arm to wave them through the door.

Lobey stomped right into the darkness, and Vidya followed, a little impressed.

"No funny business!" Lobey shouted. "Let us through, please."

Vidya followed Lobey into the dark heat of the greenhouse, the Devil's Fingers swaying gently on either side of the path. Vidya quickly caught up to Lobey. "How did you know you could do that?" she muttered to the blue-haired girl. Lobey shrugged. "Bossiness comes naturally to me, Vidya, you should know that by now." But then, in a much softer voice, she almost said to herself, "I just had this weird feeling I could."

The two girls quickly made their way through the greenhouse, squinting through the dark to find any sign of Nani. They had almost reached the back when they stopped short, Lobey gasped. Vidya strode forward to see what was going on.

Two Devil's Fingers plants had stretched out their branches to form a hammock, upon which Nani was resting comfortably with her hands folded on her tummy. One of the trees had extended a tiny branch and was slowly stroking her hair.

Vidya let out a sigh of relief. "That's lucky," she said. "Looks like they want to take care of her."

Lobey nodded, looking over the trees. "You guys look after our Nani, okay?" she said bossily. "We don't know how long this thing is going to last."

Vidya felt a pit grow in the bottom of her stomach as they turned around to make their way out of the greenhouse. How long? How long would the adults be asleep for? She shook her head. She couldn't think about that. They just had to follow her father's orders until they woke up.

They made their way back to the Palace where worried looking Fae children were streaming into the entrance hall. Some of them were crying, others had their arms around each other. Vidya's heart pounded as she thought about what she should say. As she thought about her parents and Nani, a plan slowly formed in her mind. She knew two things for sure. The first was that the Fae magic was fading. The second was that her father told her to prepare for a war, probably related to the creature that attacked Captain Silver in the Fae forest. One thing was super clear. They needed to know more. And so that's exactly what they would do. Vidya made her way through the crowd, smiling at those she knew, and made her way up the stairs where she had a good height to speak to everyone standing there.

Luna and Toad ran up the stairs when they saw her. Luna had leaf-paper and a pen in her hand.

"We've gone around making sure the adults are all okay," she muttered. "So far, everyone is accounted for. Our parents are fine, Uncle Jula-wil was found in a rose bush, so he's alright, but no one can find Uncle Billy."

Vidya nodded. Uncle Billy was her mother's younger brother.

"Just keep looking," she replied. "That's the best we can do. He's probably off in the forest somewhere."

The two triplet sisters nodded and ran back down the stairs.

The scared voices of the kids reached her, and she looked at the children of the Fae gathered in the hall. Some had babies or toddlers perched on their hips, whispering to each other, trying to understand what had happened. As Vidya stood there watching them all, she thought of baby Mahiya, sleeping soundly upstairs. She realised she needed to say something that made the kids feel safe, to make them feel she had it under control. If she were talking to Mahiya as a big sister, what would she say?

"Everybody!" She called down to them. She saw Lobey and Toad walking around the crowd, telling everybody to be quiet.

"Princess Vidya is speaking!" said Lobey loudly. "Shut up, everybody!"

As more than a hundred little eyes turned to look at her, Vidya took a deep breath.

"As you all know, the adults have fallen into a magical sleep," she began. "For some reason, for the past couple of days, the Fae magic has been fading. Yesterday, my Nani, the queen's mother, told me that kids have the strongest Fae magic, so that must be why the grown- ups are asleep and we're not."

Wings fluttered nervously below her, and somewhere, a baby squealed. Fae magic had never been known to fade before. Their magic was as sure as the sun rising every morning.

"How!" cried somebody she couldn't see. "How could Fae magic fade away?"

Anxious talking broke out.

"Listen!" she shouted. Slowly, they quietened down. "I have an idea why. First, I need the oldest kids to come to me after this meeting. Since the grown-ups are not here, it'll be up to us to sort this out. Second!" she said loudly as more whispering began. "I need the older kids to look after the younger kids and babies. Do the same things you do every day. Make sure you eat, make sure you feed the babies and change them. Got it?"

Irritated grumbles came from the crowd. "To make sure," she called over the noise. "The Lady Lobelia, Lady Lunaria and Lady Linaria, will come around to each of your houses and will check on you all while I take care of our problem. Those who aren't doing what they're told will be in big trouble when the grownups wake up. Got it?"

Vidya scanned the crowd, meeting as many pairs of eyes as she could to show she meant business. She received nods and small smiles in return. Nodding back, she finished. "Okay, the third thing is, I need anyone who knows their guardian plant to collect as much of their herbs, berries, and leaves, as possible, whatever is useful. I'm going to send Lady Lobelia out with a piece of leaf-paper to mark down who has what guardian plant so see if we can use it in some way."

Vidya sighed and nodded encouragingly at them all. "We'll have this sorted, don't worry. Now, I need the oldest kids up here. You can all go."

That was good, Vidya thought to herself. *I think father would have done it the same way.*

The crowd dispersed, and she noticed Toad directing the kids out safely while Lobey gathered up the eldest of the kids.

Vidya waited as Lobey led a small group up the stairs to her. "I've sent Luna and Toad down to the city," she said. "Here are the oldest kids."

Fifteen Fae kids, a year or two older than Vidya, lined up in front of her, one of them was Willow.

"Here's the thing," she said slowly, looking them all each in the eye. "I don't want the little kids knowing this, but the Fae forest has a big problem. There is a… creature roaming around, defying the King's Law and attacking Fae."

Their mouths dropped open in shock, wings

twitching anxiously. They knew as well as she did this was a *very* bad thing.

"We're safe on this side of the bottomless sky, of course," she assured them. "But they seem to think it's linked to the Fae magic draining. The King… the king told me to prepare for a war."

She was met by stunned silence.

Willow was the first to speak. "We are Fae, Vidya," he said slowly. "War is something we do not do."

Vidya swallowed. "These are the words from my father, the King, Willow. Lobey heard it too."

"I did," said Lobey, lifting her chin. "He said to prepare for war."

Willow made a small 'o' with his mouth. "Maybe he meant we should *prepare* for it. As in, defend the palace, right? Not to go out… and hurt whatever it is."

Vidya chewed on her lip briefly. Perhaps Willow was right. Her father had said 'prepare,' not 'go and fight a war.' "We need more information," said Vidya. "What I need is to make sure you all know what we're in for. Do what you think preparing for war means."

They all looked at each other uncertainly. What *did* preparing for war mean?

"Weapons," said Lobey, thinking out loud. "Bows and arrows."

"And food," said an older girl with yellow wings, "Collect all that sort of stuff."

Vidya nodded. "Good ideas, everyone. By the time anything happens, I'm sure the adults will wake back up and tell us what to do."

There were nods all around. But in the back of

Vidya's mind, Uncle Jula-wil's wispy voice sounded in her brain. *Darkness approaches*. First, the Fae magic was fading. Now the adults were asleep. What came next?

"Lobey made a good point," said Vidya. "We are Fae children. If we are harmed, we are allowed to defend ourselves."

The group replied with nods. Of course, they all knew this rule.

"But hopefully we don't need to," said Willow.

"Right," confirmed Vidya. "So… Willow, you're the best with an arrow, we need anyone who knows how to start making some bows and arrows and get practising with them. Can you be in charge of that?"

Willow nodded unhappily, and Vidya looked out at the rest of them.

"Alright, so what are your names, and what are you good at?" she asked. One by one, each Fae stepped forward and told her their name and if they had any skills yet. One was good at tracking, another was good at boiling potions, another was the fastest in her class. Lobey wrote them down on a piece of leaf-paper.

"Great, so we'll keep all this in mind… and in the coming days, we'll see what use we have for each one of you. Everyone will need to pitch in. It's just us, after all."

Vidya took a deep breath. She was really just making all this up as she went along. Fifteen pairs of eyes looked back at her. What next?

She was saved from her thoughts as a magical wind whipped through the air, making all their wings flutter. Vidya turned to look through an open window in the wall to her right where a green leaf spun and danced its way through the air. She stepped toward it and grabbed it quickly. She saw her own writing, then turned it over to read the reply.

She grinned. Finally, something she could count on.

"But first," she said. "Tomorrow at dawn, I'll choose a couple of you to come with me to escort Princess Sonakshi through the portal."

5

THE UNICORN PRINCESS

"The Fae have many friends in the secret parts of the world; other creatures who sing the same song but with a different melody. When we recognise the song, we know we have a true friend, a knower of the same secrets, a believer with the same heart."

—The Book of the Fae, Queen Mab the First, 3333 B.C.

Vidya awoke before the sun the next day and set out to meet the team she had chosen to come with her to collect Princess Sonakshi.

Her leaf-message had been simple.

Emergency. Fae adults ALL asleep. Need help.

Princess Sonakshi's hurried scribble was just as short.

I'll be at the portal at dawn.

Vidya's heart had swelled with joy reading her best friend's response. Sonakshi was coming to help so quickly, without question. Unicorns were special creatures, that was for sure. Since the dawn of time, the Fae and unicorns had been loyal friends. But as time went on and the unicorns decreased, the Fae had been without unicorn friends for over a hundred years. And then Princess Sonakshi had been born, and the Fae wept with happiness.

Vidya just knew that Sonakshi could help them somehow. A few months ago, they had met on Sonakshi's quest to save her friend Rowen from the evil witch Mankini. Vidya had been alerted by her people that there was a unicorn trapped in the bush. She had known immediately that the poachers Gary and George would be responsible and set out to save Sonakshi and her friends. Being the only known unicorn in existence, Vidya and Sonakshi became fast friends, writing to each other often. Sonakshi had some wonderful powers as a unicorn, including the power of healing, so Vidya was certain Sonakshi would have some ideas about how to get the Fae magic back and wake up the grown-ups.

The previous night, Vidya and Lobey had gone through the list of older kids and their skills.

She picked out three of them.

"Willow, I already know your eyes are the best, you need to come with me," she said, tapping her finger against her chin. He gave her a wide-eyed look that said he was nervous, but she continued on and chose a tall boy named Lotus whose muscles had started to take shape already. He must've been nearly thirteen. Then she picked out an orange-winged girl named Lily, who said she was the best tracker of the city kids.

She took Willow, Lotus, and Lily into a side room with chairs and asked them to sit. Confused, they hung on her every word as she laid out the plan for how they would safely escort Princess Sonakshi up to the palace and back out again. She then told them all to get to bed early that night so they could meet bright and early the next morning.

They awaited Vidya at the front of the palace. Bold Lotus, serious Willow with his bow slung over his shoulder, and the easy-going Lily. The cool morning air blew in their faces, waking them up in the dim light.

"Right, everyone!" said Vidya, clapping her hands once. "Let's go. Stay sharp."

They lifted off into the sky in a V formation with Vidya at the front, Willow and Lily slightly behind to her left and right and Lotus bringing up the rear.

They fluttered over the Bottomless Sky quickly, keeping their eyes on the line of trees on the other side, watching for any unusual movements. Vidya was not exactly sure where Captain Silver had been attacked, so in her eyes, any part of the Fae forest could be dangerous.

The forest was divided into two sections. The tree

line all along the edge of the cliff was the safe zone for the Fae. They were allowed to wander freely in this section and in and out of the portal trees that led to the human realm. If they wandered further in for a little while, pretty soon they'd would come to trees with X markings made by the Kings of old. This was the end of the safe zone, telling all Fae that to wander across into that part of the Fae forest meant danger and peril. The most dangerous creatures lived in that section, which was much bigger than the safe zone, but every so often, creatures trundled across, looking for trouble. Just like when Aunty Sandy had her nose stolen by the Yarama. So even though the team would be staying in the safe zone, Vidya was ready for anything. She wouldn't let any of them, including Princess Sonakshi, get hurt.

They touched down on the other side, enjoying the shade of the tall trees. The air smelled sweet with a mix of the banksias and eucalyptus that grew in this area.

Sipping on Ghostberry juice, they trekked through the long grass through the forest, scanning the area all around for signs of trouble.

"Worms!" chirped a bird high in a gum tree.

"Fae!" chirped another.

Vidya rolled her eyes and groaned. Clearly, the birds had not lost the Fae magic that made them speak English.

"Shh!" she said into the trees, pressing a finger into her lips.

Next to her, Willow shook his head, navy wings

quivering slightly. "At least they'll announce any strange creature nearby," he said helpfully.

"I hope so," she said as a magpie warbled loudly:

"Dawn is approaching!"

They stomped through the otherwise quiet forest for a few minutes, finally arriving at the great portal tree. This portal was made of Eucalyptus and was the closest one to Sonakshi's secret home in the Blue Mountains. The tall trees shaded them from the rising sun as Vidya touched a finger to the portal tree, making it flash bright gold light. A door formed in the wooden trunk, and it opened, swinging outward toward her, and Vidya stepped through into the human realm.

"Princess Vidya!" came an excited cry.

Vidya turned to her left and saw Princess Sonakshi standing there in her human form, her black as night hair swinging as she ran toward Vidya.

"Princess Sonakshi!" she called, and the two girls embraced each other. "Oh, hello King Deven," added Vidya, seeing Sonakshi's father making his way through the bush behind her. A couple of guards waited further away on the path. Sonakshi, being a unicorn, could see her easily, but the ghostberry juice Vidya was drinking made king Deven squint through the dawn light to see her properly.

"Thank you for coming," Vidya said.

"We were so worried to read your message," said Sonakshi. "What's happened?"

"Something has happened to the Fae magic. We're trying to figure it out. First the plants started dying, then we woke up yesterday morning to find we couldn't wake the adults. It looks like they're in some type of magical sleep. My father spoke to me before he slept. He told me to prepare for a war!"

King Deven gave her a worried look. "This isn't sounding good, Vidya," he said in a low voice. "If your father is telling you to prepare for a war, this is serious."

Vidya nodded. "We have to fix this, King Deven, I just have to figure out how. I'm sorry I can't take you through. But my guard and I will return Sona in a couple of hours if that's okay?"

He nodded. "I don't like this, girls. Sonakshi, I don't want you spending too much time in there."

"We won't keep her long then," said Vidya quickly. "I just want to see if any unicorn magic can wake my father up or… do anything to help us, really. We don't know what else to do. It's just us Fae kids now."

Deven nodded, "Be quick and be careful. My men and I will wait here."

"Thanks, father," said Sonakshi, and hand in hand, the two girls walked through the portal tree where the others were anxiously waiting.

Vidya shut the portal door behind them and quickly introduced Sonakshi to the others, who came forward to shake her hand vigorously, staring at her golden eyes.

"Lovely to meet you all," said Sonakshi formally, "I just wish it was under better circumstances."

They nodded glumly.

"Let's head off," said Vidya. "I don't want to spend

any more time in the forest than we have to."

As they trekked back through the forest, Sonakshi chatted excitedly. "I wanted to fly as soon as I got your message," she said, magnificent golden unicorn eyes meeting Vidya's green Fae ones. "But my father said it would be too dangerous. I'm still not allowed to fly out of the castle grounds, really. I'll be so glad to transform here."

Sonakshi looked around the Fae forest and breathed in deeply, frowning. "It feels different from last time," she said, looking left and right.

Vidya nodded as they walked at the centre of the group this time, Willow and Lily at the front, Lotus at the back. "It *is* different," replied Vidya. "It's really worrying, but all I can do is try to figure it out one step at a time until the adults wake up."

Sonakshi nodded. "I hope I can help. I do enjoy getting your messenger-leaves every week. Is Mahiya still giving away sparks with every fart?"

Vidya giggled, and Pancake finally woke up and emerged out of her pocket to see where the unfamiliar voice was coming from.

"Yes, with every burp as well. This is Pancake. He's a quokka."

Sonakshi gasped and reached for Pancake, who stared at her with his mouth hanging open. Pancake reached for her, and soon he was in her arms, gazing up into her eyes with wonder.

"He's never seen a unicorn before," laughed Vidya.

"Well, you wait," laughed Sonakshi back. "I haven't even turned into my unicorn self yet."

Pancake sat in Sonakshi's hands, staring at her honey-coloured face as they walked through the forest. Soon, they reached the edge of the cliff, and Sonakshi handed Pancake back to Vidya. She exploded in a thrill of golden light, and before they knew it, Vidya and the other kids were grinning at Sonakshi's golden eyes in her unicorn form. Lily let out an excited "Ooh!"

She was the colour of silvery moonlight, with opalescent wings tucked by her side and a glittering diamond horn that caught the light, making it sparkle magically. Pancake squealed when he saw Sonakshi, and gasped, pointing a clawed finger at her and jumping up and down in Vidya's arms.

With a whoop of joy, Sonakshi gave two powerful downward strokes of her wings and leapt into the air. Vidya and the other Fae kids laughed at the sight of her having such joy at flying in the open air. They followed quickly after, fluttering their wings rapidly to keep up with her.

Vidya met Sonakshi on the other side. The other girl had transformed back into her human self, and the group rushed into the palace, Pancake chattering excitedly.

Vidya wasted no time. She led Sonakshi immediately up to her parents' room first and found Toad and Luna in there, shrieking as baby Mahiya, lying on her change table, let out an almighty *squelch.* The two girls screamed. Toad held a loose nappy over Mahiya, but her head was turned away and screwed up in a grimace. Vidya watched in horror as a bright red spark flew from Mahiya's hands, through the air, and onto Luna's dress. The girl looked down as her dress caught alight, and she screamed, slapping herself to get the flame out.

"Oh, mother earth!" Toad cried.

Vidya and Sonakshi burst into a fit of laughter at the scene, and Toad groaned loudly at them.

"*You* try to change this one's nappy!" she grumbled loudly, leaning down to get a clean nappy. "There's *always* poo and fire everywhere!"

"Thanks, Toad," laughed Vidya, wiping her eyes. "I'll do the next one."

"No, it's okay," said Toad, fastening the new nappy on, then lifting baby Mahiya and planting a kiss on her cheek. "I'm getting good at it now. Besides, you're busy saving the Kingdom."

She turned, and upon seeing Sonakshi, froze on the spot, baby Mahiya gurgled in the air.

"Are you—?" Toad began.

"Hello," said Sonakshi. "I'm Sonakshi."

"The unicorn Princess!" cried Luna, her mouth hanging open.

"Yes," said Vidya, dragging Sonakshi past Luna and toward the bed where her mother lay. "She's here to see if her magic will do anything for our problem."

"Right," said Sonakshi, nodding. "Stand back everyone."

The three girls, with Toad holding baby Mahiya, moved right back to the edge of the room.

Sonakshi shook herself, and in a flash and a gasp

from Luna and Toad, turned into her unicorn form. The three girls watched as Sonakshi carefully lowered her glittering diamond horn onto Queen Salote. Her horn touched the queen's forehead and flashed brightly where it met her skin. Queen Salote coughed once, then rolled onto her side and kept on sleeping.

Vidya groaned. "That's okay, Sona, try my father next, he's lying on the floor on the other side."

Sonakshi carefully walked around the bed, and the girls followed to watch. She repeated the move, but this time, the King gasped loudly, his eyes opening, looking around widely.

"Father!" Vidya rushed forward.

King Farrion grasped onto Vidya's arm and looked her right in the eyes.

"They are taking the Fae magic, Vidya!" he cried out. "They are taking it!"

"Who is?" Vidya cried.

But the King immediately let go of her arm, head falling back onto the carpet with a thump, and began snoring once again.

"Do it again, Sona!" cried Vidya. "Do it again!"

Sonakshi hurriedly leaned down again, but this time, after the bright flash of light, the King did not stir.

Vidya stood, breathing shakily. She ran her hands through her magenta hair and leaned on Sonakshi for support. The unicorn Princess nuzzled Vidya's neck comfortingly. Pancake scrambled up to Vidya's shoulder, patting the girl's face.

"That was scary," said Toad, patting baby Mahiya on

the back. "At least it worked for a moment."

"What do you think he meant?" asked Luna.

Vidya straightened and shook her head. "Someone is stealing the Fae magic. We all heard him."

"How could that be?" asked Luna. "How do you steal it?"

"Magic is a funny thing," said Sonakshi with a distant look in her eye. She flashed back into her human form and looked down at King Farrion, snoring peacefully now. "The witch Mankini tried to steal my magic through my blood. And she almost did it." Sonakshi shivered.

"Fae is magic is different," said Vidya thoughtfully. "But not that different. Our magic comes from the earth, we just have to figure out how somebody is draining it."

Sonakshi blew air out of her mouth. "You'd better find out soon," she said. "This type of thing can't go on forever. What if they drain it completely?"

The three Fae girls looked at each other with worry. "We'll find out," Vidya said, more confidently than she felt.

"The Fae King has the strongest magic of the adults," mused Sonakshi. "I could feel the difference. Not enough to keep him awake, but enough that I could wake him for a second. I'm guessing that's why he was the last adult to go to sleep in the first place."

"Hopefully, that means he's the first to wake up then," said Vidya.

* * *

Vidya led Sonakshi out of the bedroom and back down the stairs into the great dining room where a few kids were sitting eating some food they had clumsily prepared. The two Princesses went to join them.

"Baby Mahiya is so cute," said Sonakshi, inspecting a glass of ghostberry juice. "I'm glad I got to meet her."

"We're still trying to figure out where the sparks come from," said Vidya. "No other Fae babies do it."

Sonakshi cocked her head to the side. "When I look at her, I think of… lava. Like the stuff that's deep inside the earth."

Vidya shook her head. "That mystery will have to wait until this is over. I have bigger things to worry about than Mahiya farting."

Sonakshi giggled, and Vidya couldn't help but do the same.

The two girls sat deep in thought with Pancake sitting between them, eating a strawberry.

"I'm sorry it didn't work more, Vidya," said Sonakshi sadly. "I really thought it would. A unicorn's horn is supposed to be the most powerful healing tool in the world. I've used it heaps since I discovered that."

"I guess the Fae magic can't be healed that way," said Vidya, softly.

"Oh, I almost forgot," Sonakshi fished into her purple backpack and brought out a tiny glass container with swirling silver liquid inside. "I collected some tears for you." She handed the container over, and Vidya held it in her hand, staring at it curiously.

"Your tears are silver?" she asked.

"Yeah, who would've thought, hey? But anyway, the

point is, my tears are useful, swallow them and they give you unicorn powers for a short period of time. So, I was thinking if you needed it for healing, or flying faster… it could be of use."

"Wow," Vidya said. "That's a brilliant idea, thank you for that."

"No worries."

"I just never thought anything like this could happen, Sona," said Vidya wistfully, staring at the silvery liquid. "The Fae magic is as sure as the sun. What if it goes away completely?"

Sonakshi absently patted Pancake on the head.

"You'll do what you do best, Vidya. You'll read, you'll think, and you'll figure it out."

Vidya looked at her unicorn friend in appreciation and nodded. She had just really hoped Sonakshi could fix this situation, but she should've known it was all bigger than that.

"You're more than a friend to me, Sona," Vidya said. "You're a sister."

Sonakshi burst into tears and threw her arms around Vidya.

"Please let me know what happens," Sonakshi said, releasing her as Pancake squeaked in protest as he got squashed between the two girls.

"Here, take these." Vidya took out a bunch of messenger leaves from her pocket and handed them over. "Then you can write to me whenever you like."

"Let me know if we can help anymore," Sonakshi said. "Father has plenty of guards—"

"Human grown-ups can't come in here," reminded

Vidya, shaking her head. "And I don't want you to get caught up in anything dangerous here."

Suddenly, the kids next to them let out a cheer, and the two girls looked at where they were pointing.

Daisy and Luna emerged from the palace kitchens holding two large cakes.

"It's not burnt!" said Daisy proudly.

"Well, it is a little," admitted Luna, plonking hers down on the table. "But its covered in icing, so that's okay, right?"

"Right," nodded Daisy. "Mum's gonna be so proud of me, when she wakes up, I'm going to be an excellent cook!"

"Just whatever you do," said a boy with spotted black and white wings. "Please don't make that *thing* you made last night again."

"Excuse me," Daisy said, affronted. "I thought that was a lovely broccoli stew!"

The kids made gagging noises.

Vidya shook her head. The Fae kids were doing well without their parents so far, with the older kids making sure no one burnt the place down, but, reminded herself, it *had* only been a day and a half.

After feeding Sonakshi cake and the green mess Daisy called 'broccoli stew', Vidya rounded up the team again, and before long, they were flying toward the Fae forest. Landing, Sonakshi turned back into human form, and they trudged through the trees.

They had been walking for ten minutes when Sonakshi stopped and turned to peer into the dark forest.

"Did you hear that?" she frowned.

The others stopped and listened.

"I can't hear anything," said Vidya, scratching Pancake's head where he sat in her pocket.

Sonakshi shrugged. "My unicorn hearing reaches a super long way away, so it could've just been a platypus in that billabong a few kilometres away."

They continued walking, but within two seconds, Vidya heard it too.

"I heard that!" Vidya exclaimed, peering in the forest. "It sounded just like someone was saying—"

"OI!"

Vidya jumped and immediately turned, heading in the direction of the voice. Willow and Sonakshi called for her to stop, but Vidya pushed through the bushes into the dark of the forest. That voice did not seem sinister, it had seemed sort of nasally. Vidya felt Sonakshi close behind her, followed by the angry grumbles of Lily and Willow.

Vidya stormed through a line of bushes and found herself in front of a Fae pond. She knew it was a Fae pond and not a regular pond because of the way the blue water glowed with its own light. It was small enough that Vidya could've jumped over it easily. There were many Fae ponds all over the Fae realm. They had been created by the first living Fae as a connection to the merpeople of the great oceans of the world. Through a Fae pond, a mermaid or merman could swim up from the ocean and speak to the Fae. They were supposed to be tricky to find out in the ocean. It took real skill for a merperson to find them, let alone the right one. But it was something that was passed down to children from their parents. But it was not the Fae pond that caught Vidya's attention; it was what was next to the pond.

Sitting on a large wet rock next to the pond was the strangest creature she had ever seen. He was some sort of fish, except he was fat and blob-like. It reminded Vidya of a sunken ball of jelly, and she had certainly never seen a fish with a nose that big and fat before. He stared at them back in an unimpressed sort of way with bored, black eyes. Then, to her shock, he opened his mouth and spoke.

"I have a message," his voice was nasally, like his nose was blocked due to allergies, and he droned as if he was very annoyed at having to be there.

Vidya and Sonakshi stared at him. The others gathered into the clearing.

"*I said*, I have a message," the fish repeated, annoyed. Vidya had never spoken to a fish before, but his lips were definitely moving. Animals of the Fae spoke all the time. She supposed fish that lived near merpeople probably could talk as well.

Vidya stepped forward hastily, "Yes, sorry, sir, I didn't hear you properly."

"Yes. Well, I'm in a hurry. It's for the Princess of the Fae." He squinted at her. "Are you the Princess of the Fae?"

"I'm Princess Vidya, yes. And this is Princess

Sonakshi."

The fish's black eyes widened at this, and he gave what looked like a nod, but it was more like a twitch because he did not have a head to nod.

"I have heard of you," he said to Sonakshi. "Her royal watery-ness, Princess Meera of the Western Pacific merpeople has an important message," he droned on.

"Princess Meera sent you?" asked Sonakshi. She turned to Vidya. "I met her on the way to Fiji. She saved the boat you loaned me from capsizing, Vidya."

The fish twitched again.

"Yes. Well. The message is this: *Emergency. Bunyip sighting near the Fae pond. Eating creatures. Be careful. Investigating now. I've sent Bob to tell you.*" He flapped a small fin. "Bob is me."

"A Bunyip?" said Lotus in disbelief. He crossed his arms. "There has not been a Bunyip here since King Fern and Queen Talia of the merpeople locked them up two hundred years ago."

Bob twitched. "It appears that they have woken up. From the magical spell laid on them."

"All of them?" asked Vidya, "How many are there exactly?"

Lotus shook his head "It's just not possible, Vidya. I highly doubt—"

"I mean, it could be true," interrupted Willow. "Vidya, do you remember what Master Sunny—"

A roar pierced the air. A terrifying, spine tingling, heavy sound that made the earth beneath them tremble.

Vidya's heart froze in her chest.

"Oh no," Bob droned, "They're coming!"

It was Lotus who sprang into action first, "Princess Sonakshi, to the portal, now!"

Vidya thought fast, and she whipped out a messenger leaf and jammed into Bob's mouth.

"For Meera to send me a message later," she blurted.

Sonakshi and Vidya then bolted, hearing a splash as Bob must have flopped back into the water. Pancake shrieked on Vidya's shoulder, and she hoped he held on tight as the two Princesses and the three Fae kids sprinted through the bush, dodging branches and jumping over logs.

Vidya and the other Fae propelled themselves forward even faster, using their wings. Vidya grasped Sonakshi's hand, dragging her forward.

"We're close!" she cried and veered left, Sonakshi panting behind her.

Vidya spotted the portal tree in the distance. "There!"

They jumped over another log and cleared a bush, and Vidya stuck her finger into the trunk, drawing the doorway. Light flashed, and she grabbed the doorknob just as it appeared. Vidya pushed Sonakshi forward at the same time she pushed the door open. As soon as Sonakshi was through, Vidya slammed the door shut. A scream came from behind her, and Vidya turned to see Lotus, also turning to see who had screamed. A black hulking figure threw Lily through the air. The small girl spun in the air but flapped her wings and rose, flying into the trees. Vidya's heart stopped. The beast thundering through the bushes was black with sleek skin from the neck down and four muscled legs. It rose onto its hind legs and roared from a mouth like an enormous dog with huge sharp yellow canine teeth. He stared at them all with huge, angry eyes. It was exactly like the creature in the book Master Sunny had shown them.

"Fly!" Lotus shouted taking a running jump. "Fly!"

Vidya and the others shot into the air as another earth-shattering roar filled their ears. Pancake screamed, and Vidya caught him just as he tumbled off her shoulder. She stuffed him into her pocket, and, panting, she met the four others above the treetops.

"Bunyip!" cried Willow, supporting a slumped Lily. She cradled one of her arms and winced in pain. "It's really a bunyip!" The trees beneath them shook as the Bunyip tried to climb up.

"Back to the palace!" cried Vidya. "Go, go, go!"

Princess Sonakshi stumbled through the portal tree. She turned around and just managed to get a view of what was behind Vidya before she slammed the door shut. That creature was horrifying. She called out with a sob.

"Father!"

She stumbled through the forest, not believing what she had seen. She could see her father and her guards camped through the trees.

"Father!"

King Devin jumped up from his seat on the log and, seeing Sonakshi through the trees, he ran to grab her.

"What happened Sona? Are you okay?"

Sonakshi huddled into her father's arms and heard the rushed footsteps of Captain Sampson and his men.

"What happened?" her father repeated.

"M-monster." Was all she could say. "I hope Vidya and the others flew away safely."

"You're safe now, love."

He patted her on the back, and she felt calmed instantly. She was safe here, that… Bunyip couldn't get through. The portal was closed.

She stepped away from her father and wiped her eyes.

"The mermaid Princess Meera sent a message through the Fae pond," she explained. "And then we saw it—it chased us. They said it was called a Bunyip."

Her father's brown face changed completely. It went an ashen colour, and he took a sharp breath. He took her hand and walked her back to the camp. The guards followed.

"Pack up everything Sampson," he said in a grave voice. He turned back to Sonakshi.

"Listen, Sona. After we rescued Rowen from Mank-ini's island, I had all of her things collected from her witch's tower. Papers, books, instruments, everything. I didn't want anyone finding and using the information she had stored there. I brought it all back with us and read some of it."

He took a deep breath and shook his head. "If what I've read is true, then the Fae are in great danger."

6

OLD ENEMIES

"Why does the sky cry sometimes? "

"The sky cries as a mother does, when she thinks about how much she loves her children. And through her love, her children grow and are fed and live happy lives."

—Queen Salote to Princess Vidya

Princess Sonakshi returned to her castle in the Blue Mountains by nightfall, guarded carefully by her father, Captain Sampson, and the guards. It was a hidden place, as King Deven and Queen Ria had escaped Fiji seven years earlier, hiding Sonakshi, then a baby unicorn, from the cunning witch Mankini. The old witch had needed Sonakshi's blood for a spell that would reverse a curse she had gotten by killing Sonakshi's grandfather, also a unicorn. In the end, Mankini had resorted to kidnapping Sonakshi's best friend, Rowen, to lure her to her tower in Makogai. It had worked, but Sonakshi had gotten the better of Mankini. The witch turned to dust, and Sonakshi had learned what it meant to be a unicorn.

Hidden away in the Blue Mountains, their closest neighbours were the Lord and Lady of Cabbage Tree Creek, so their children, Kiera and Rowen, had become Sonakshi's best friends.

"Sona!" cried Kiera, running down the palace stairs, her flaming red hair streaming behind her.

"You're back!" cried Rowen, three years younger, but just as fast at running as his sister.

Sonakshi grinned when she saw the two of them, puffing and panting down the stairs. "You guys won't believe it!" she said. "Wait till I tell you—"

"I want all of you in bed," ordered King Deven. "We will talk to Batuman tomorrow."

"Batuman?" asked Kiera, wrinkling her nose. "Why do we have to talk to *him*?"

The obese bat had been Mankini's servant. They had brought him back with them from Fiji and locked him in the dungeons beneath the castle because King Deven had wanted to keep a close eye on him.

"I'll tell you everything," said Sonakshi, leading her two friends up the stairs and to their rooms. The two often slept over at the castle, as they all went to school together with the children of the guards who also lived there. The three kids sat in Sonakshi's room with their pyjamas on, gasping in shock as Sonakshi told them about her escape from the Bunyip.

"On the way back, I got a messenger leaf from

Vidya saying she got home safely. I was so worried. That thing was so scary."

Yawning, and content they had just listened to one of the most daring stories they had ever heard, they pulled up the covers of Sonakshi's bed, and all fell asleep.

The next morning, King Deven took the three of them down the long stairs that led below the castle, into the dark of the dungeons. Rowen tightly clutched onto Kiera's hand. He had been locked up in Mankini's dungeon in Fiji for days, and seeing these dungeons reminded him about that awful time.

Sonakshi was thinking about her own feelings. Batuman had helped Mankini do some horrible things, including lie to her and kidnap Rowen. He had also hurt people, including herself and her grandfather. The old bat had cried the entire way from Fiji, mourning the loss of his Mistress. He and Mankini had been together for a hundred years, so it was fair that he would be upset about the whole thing. But Sonakshi wasn't entirely sure he was deserving of a life imprisonment for his crimes either, there was magic keeping him alive for an artificially long time after all. Mankini might have died, but her magic had lived on. Who knows how long he would live for? Did he deserve forever in this jail cell? They took him out once a day for walks, but he was not allowed to fly. Sonakshi imagined being told that she could never ever fly again and shivered at the thought. There would be nothing worse, she decided. Flying was who she was.

They followed her father down a long dark corridor, past a line of three empty cells. They kept Batuman in the last one.

They found him lying on his tiny bed made of soft linen. He had propped himself up with pillows and was engrossed in an old book. A bowl of water was off to one side, and a punnet of berries. When he saw the group step in front of his cell, he gasped and jumped off his bed, dropping the book to the floor with a clatter.

"Princess Sonakshi!" he cried, waddling up to the bars of the cell. He clasped his hands in front of him, bowing low. "Your majesty."

The children stood in a line against the bars of the cell, King Devin took a seat on a stool just behind them.

"Oh, little Rowen, and friend too!" he said lightly.

"Hello Batuman," said Sonakshi in a quiet voice.

Kiera and Rowen remained silent, glowering at him. Neither had quite forgiven him for his part in Rowen's kidnapping and Sonakshi's near death.

"Oh, hello Unicorn Princess, Batuman is so happy that you've come to see him!" Batuman bounced on the balls of his feet.

"Are you well, Batuman?"

"Oh yes, your Majesty, very well in this dark dungeon. The guards bring me little fruits to eat. And Scotch Finger biscuits. Yes, those are Batuman's favourites."

Sonakshi nodded. "Well, we've come to see you because we need your help."

"Oh yes?" He clapped his hands eagerly. "Batuman is happy to help however he can."

"My father has found something in Mankini's documents. She mentions the Bunyips quite a bit."

Batuman's face fell, the corners of his mouth drooping. He stopped bouncing on his feet and became rather still.

"Oh dear. Yes. That."

"That?" asked Sonakshi, nervously toying with the metal bar in front of her.

"I mean… Batuman knows nothing!" he squeezed his black lips hard together and shook his head so vigorously back-and-forth Sonakshi thought he might do some damage to his brain.

"Batuman," she cooed disapprovingly. "Please tell us what you know."

The old bat sighed, looking at his feet, his tiny round belly expanding like a balloon as he breathed in and out. "Batuman does not know what to say."

"Start with the truth!" Kiera slapped the bars with a hand, her temper getting the better of her.

Batuman jumped back in shock. "Excuse me!"

"Batuman," hissed Kiera, fists clenched, turning the colour of a strawberry. "Do not think we have forgotten what you did to Rowen!" She pressed her face against the cold iron bars. "*You owe us.*"

Batuman burst into tears. "B- Batuman is s-sorry!"

He wailed and threw himself face first onto the floor.

Kiera scoffed and pulled Rowen back to go and stand further away with King Deven, who put a reassuring arm around the little boy.

"Come on, Batuman," said Sonakshi gently. "Kiera is correct, we have the right to know everything."

Batuman quietened and pulled himself off the floor with a huff and a rather long groan. He wiped his eyes and sniffed, staring up at Sonakshi.

"Batuman is really sorry, unicorn Princess. He will serve you now."

Sonakshi nodded and gave him a small smile.

"Now, why would Mankini be writing about Bunyips in her books? They are native to Australia, right? Not Fiji."

Batuman nodded earnestly.

"Don't think that a powerful person like Mankini springs up out of nowhere," he said in a thick voice. "She comes from a long line of dark witches. When witches have children, sometimes they turn out a bit… different."

"Like a slippery man-eating beast different?" called Kiera from behind Sonakshi.

Batuman ignored her.

"Mankini has two brothers. The elder one happens to be called the Bunyip King."

An icy fist took hold of Sonakshi's heart. *The Bunyip King.*

"But there have not been Bunyips sighted for decades," said King Deven.

Batuman nodded.

"Ahh, yes. And did anyone wonder why that is?"

Batuman held up a fat finger. "How did the Bunyips go from gobbling up humans left right and centre, to just —" he clicked his batty fingers. "Nothing. The answer, your unicorn highness… is. The. Fae."

Sonakshi frowned. Where was this story going?

"The Fae are the custodians of the land. They keep the balance. When they saw how powerful the terrifying Bunyips were getting, how many humans were getting eaten, they had to do something."

Sonakshi glanced back at her father, who was frowning at Batuman now.

"With the help of the Queen of the merpeople," said Batuman, stepping forward. "Princess Vidya's grandfather, King Fern, rounded up all the Bunyips."

He paused for effect.

"But the Fae do not harm living things," he jeered. "So they did the cleverest thing. They locked up the Bunyips and their King, in a cave in the Fae lands. In that cave where the only water supply was a deep pool of sleeping potion."

Sonakshi found it suddenly hard to breathe. Was it possible that Vidya's grandfather had done this? Batuman must have seen the scepticism on her face because he quickly added. "You were not there, unicorn majesty, the Bunyips were taking *everybody*. Eating everyone they could find. The Fae King could not leave monsters roaming around the Murray river. He had to fix it."

"Alright," came King Deven's voice. "If that's the case, then how does Mankini come into it?"

Batuman stepped forward. "Mankini wanted

revenge for what the Fae had done to her brother and his people. It was her life's mission after... collecting my unicorn mistress, of course." He bowed at Sonakshi again.

A jolt of old fear struck Sonakshi, but she remembered Mankini was dust now. She was not alive to get her revenge on the Fae.

"But she's gone now."

"Not quite," said Batuman, holding up a fat finger.

Sonakshi stared at him in horror. She had seen Mankini die before her eyes. Seen her turn to dust and fade away. Sonakshi had broken the curse herself!

"Mankini may be gone in body, but her spells still remain, do they not?" Batuman bowed, indicating himself as the truth of the matter. *He* was still alive after a hundred odd years, after all.

"And this spell was a spell of a special kind. On the event of her death, the spell would activate, and the Bunyip King would awaken, and he would be sent special knowledge of how to take his revenge."

Batuman shrugged his furry shoulders. "And that's all I know."

Sonakshi remembered Mankini's last words to her in her tower on Makogai Island. *There will be others*. It sent a shiver up her spine. She meant *this*. She meant her brother. But they weren't coming for her. They were coming for all the Fae.

King Deven stood. "We must warn the Fae, Sona."

Sonakshi nodded, and the small group made their way out of the dungeons. But a thought in the back of her mind made Sonakshi linger behind.

"Batuman…" she said, coming to stand in front of the cage again. Batuman was sitting on his bed, toying with his blankets. He looked up with hopeful eyes. "You said Mankini had two brothers?"

He nodded his fat head.

"What do you know about the other brother? The one that's not a Bunyip?"

Batuman shrugged one shoulder and looked down at his feet. "I do not know much, Princess."

She nodded, biting her lip in thought.

As Sonakshi turned her back on him to leave, she did not see the sly smile that had spread across the old bat's face.

7

THE BUNYIP KING

The Bunyip King sat on his throne of rocks, staring at the forest around him. His bunyip army had built a bonfire in the middle of the clearing that they called their current home. Behind him was the cave where they had slept for over one hundred years. The large rock that had blocked it tightly shut was standing uselessly to the side. He was the biggest Bunyip of them all, and he watched the rest of them with too-clever eyes.

One group of his Bunyip army were chopping down trees to make more space. Another group was fast asleep after a long night of patrol. They had taken over this forest, and half of the silly little creatures in it had fled in fear. They owned it now.

When he first woke up weeks ago, his world had been dark and cold, his thoughts full of what had been done to him and his people. The Bunyips around him been fast asleep in their spots, still and silent. Just when he wished he never had been woken, a light had come to him through the darkness, and he had seen his sister's face. He had been so happy to see Mankini, but then she told him that the spell that allowed her to send him the message meant that she had died. His grief made him howl with sadness into the lonely dark. But then she told him what he needed to do to get his revenge for what the Fae had done to him, and it had made him feel better.

He had followed her instructions to the letter. His sister was so brilliant, so genius, that her plan was unthinkable and quite unexpected. But it had worked. He'd swum deep into the ocean. He'd fought dark sea creatures and returned with the secret weapon. The very thing he'd need to make him successful against the Fae.

His army had awoken clever. They could talk to each other properly and they could build fires. They were smarter than they had been before.

Before, that is, they had been forced into a prison of sleep. Tricked and imprisoned. The Fae were responsible for everything. Because of them, he and his people had been left for dead. His fist clenched around the rock he was holding. It crumbled to dust. It hadn't taken him much effort at all. He was now also strong. Far stronger than before his long sleep.

He had a secret. Something the tree huggers would never guess. Something they would not even think was possible.

"Those flower sniffing, tree hugging abominations!" he growled.

One of his soldiers, young and keen, came to his side.

"They're disgusting, your highness, so disgusting."

The Bunyip King growled with approval.

His eye caught movement at the edge of the forest. One of his Generals was escorting three Yara-ma-yha-who out of the line of trees. There were many strange and fearsome creatures in this forest, but out of them, the Yarama were apparently the scariest. They were small red men with bald heads and big teeth. Once they had their prey, there was no escaping.

But the Bunyip King did not find them scary at all. *His* teeth were sharper. *His* muscles were stronger. *His* brain was more clever.

The Yarama at the front was holding something in his hands as he walked toward him. The Bunyip King watched them with unimpressed eyes as they came to stand in front of where he sat.

"My King," said the general. "This is the chief of the Yarama. To thank us for our protection, he has come with a gift."

The Yarama were trembling with fear as they stood there. He knew that one Bunyip was a scary sight for creatures such as these, and as the King, he was bigger and scarier.

"What is it?" he growled, leaning down to look the Yarama in his beady little eyes.

The little man looked down quickly and gulped. He held the thing up high. The Bunyip King leaned down and sniffed at it, then wrinkled his nose.

"It stinks of the Fae."

The Yarama mumbled something.

"What did you say?" he asked, aggressively.

The Yarama jumped, then recovered and blurted, "A stolen potion, your kingliness, sir."

The Bunyip King grunted, feeling irritation boiling within him.

"What does it do?" he leaned back on his throne.

"Strengthens you—"

The Bunyip King grabbed the Yarama chief in one claw and, with little effort, hurled him straight into the trees where he had come from. The other two Yarama shrieked and scattered, running at full pelt after their chief.

Bunyips around him laughed in amusement, gravelly and deep.

A potion to increase strength? What a fool! Only the spindly legged Fae needed potions made of the stinky flowers to make them strong.

But he and his army were already the strongest things in this forest. The secret sat in the cavern behind him, filling the once dark space with golden light. He didn't even have to look at it to feel it's magic. It was so powerful that just by holding it; he had been changed for good. The best thing was, those dratted Fae wouldn't even see it coming. He sure had a few surprises for them.

He had just one problem to solve. Just one big issue. The endless sky. The Fae people had one unstoppable defence. Better than any wall or any army was the fact that the Fae palace sat in the middle of the sky. He could bring his entire army to the edge of that cliff, and they could roar all they wanted. But it would all be for nothing if they could not get across. He had thought of everything. A gigantic bridge, a catapult, some trick or clever way to get the Fae to come to them. But nothing he thought of would work. It made him so angry that this one tiny thing was stopping them. He had every other thing. He just needed the answer to this problem. Heat ran through him. His blood felt like hot lava through his body that was so fierce he wanted to rip up a tree and throw it over that gap to the palace. He wanted to tear down every tree in this horrible place. He wanted every Fae to leave this place. He needed it. It would be his. It was his. He and the Bunyips deserved it.

Every rock, every root, every flower, every bird. Every inch of soil was his. Those ugly tree huggers just didn't know it yet.

As his body fizzed and boiled with anger and desperation, a pain blasted from his back. He shouted out, roaring in anger. The other Bunyips jumped up in alarm and stopped what they were doing to stare at their King.

He crumpled to the floor with a grunt. The pain faded away. In its place, he could *feel* something on his back. He stood up from the grass and frowned at the strange sensation. Two *things* twitched on his back, and he could feel them like he could feel his arms or legs. Then he noticed his people staring at him with shocked expressions.

"What is it?" he barked at his general.

General opened his mouth but nothing came out.

"What is on my back?" he shouted, twisting around to look at it.

Then he saw what had just grown from his back, and he froze. A wide smile spread across his face. Next to him, General collapsed, crying out, clawing at his own back. The Bunyip King watched him as he writhed on the grass, and could barely contain his glee.

"This is it," he said, stepping forward and addressing his army with his arms up in the air. "We have been given the answer!"

Around him, Bunyips collapsed to the ground, clutching their backs and roaring in pain.

He was right. It was a miracle.

"Victory is ours!" shouted the general, coming to his feet, flexing his new muscles.

"Victory over the Fae!" shouted two more. The bunyips took up the chant in deep voices that shook the ground. "Victory! Victory, victory!"

8

INTO THE FOREST

Magic is the thing that exists between this and that. It is the space between here and there. Magic is the thing that makes scientists weep and makes poets burst with joy. It is the whisper that comes before dawn and the sigh that you hear in the air after dusk.

—The Book of the Fae, Queen Mab the First, 3333 B.C.

Vidya woke up to a sharp tap on her face. She sat up, rubbing her eyes. She had fallen asleep in the library, on top of the book *"The Bunyip: Sightings and Stories"*. Willow was opposite her, curled up on a chair, and Lobey was sleeping on the floor, using a heavy book as a pillow. Once they had dropped Princess Sonakshi through the portal and escaped with their lives from the attacking Bunyip, they had returned to the palace and researched as much as they could about the creatures. They had gathered up every book they could find on the subject, but the Book Tree only gave them the names of the same two books. But it didn't matter. Vidya had seen the power of the Bunyip herself. As well as his body, his eyes were strong because he had no trouble seeing them even though they'd drunk the ghostberry potion.

Pancake squeaked next to her, getting her attention.

In his paws was a messenger leaf. She quickly took it from him and read the tiny lines of black ink that was the familiar writing of Princess Sonakshi. It looked like she had tried to cram as much as she could onto the small leaf.

Talked to Batuman. Mankini's brother is Bunyip King. Father says King Fern rounded up Bunyips hundreds of years ago and put to sleep in a cave as too dangerous in the human realm. Woken by a spell set by Mankini. Want revenge against Fae.

Vidya's mind whirled. She knew about King Fern already from Master Sunny's story about the Bunyips. But the last sentence of the message made her sit up. *Revenge.* She frowned, *Mankini's brother?*

This new information whizzed around her brain.

"Willow," she called. "Lobey, wake up!"

The two kids opened sleepy eyes and yawned. Lobey stretched out on the floor, massaging her neck, frowning at the book she'd been sleeping on. The library door opened, and Toad walked in with baby Mahiya swaddled in her arms.

"Toad," said Vidya. "Gather the older kids, we need to have a meeting. I have new information."

Toad's blue eyebrows shot up, and she spun around and went straight back through the door.

When the triplets, Mahiya, Willow, Lotus, and Lily were all sitting in front of her around the table, she read out Sonakshi's message.

"This… Batuman can't be lying, could he?" asked Willow, rubbing his face.

Vidya shook her head. "No, Sonakshi wouldn't tell us this if she wasn't sure."

"The Bunyip King," said Lotus slowly. "That sounds worse than we thought."

"It sounds scary," said Toad, bouncing baby Mahiya on her lap. "If they have a King, how many of them are there?"

The room fell quiet. Then Lobey spoke.

"Enough to start a war with us."

Vidya's heart pounded in her chest. Were they going to war with the Bunyips?

"Look, we have no proof yet that the Bunyips want a war," said Willow reasonably.

"Princess Sonakshi's letter said they want revenge," pointed out Lobey, narrowing her eyes at Willow.

"The Bunyip yesterday seemed like a nasty guy," said Willow defensively. "But he seemed like a regular creature. Are they even smart enough to start a war with us?"

They all turned toward Lily, who sat rubbing her

sprained arm. "They have a King," she said softly. "Then they are smart."

"It doesn't matter though," said Willow, shaking his head. "The bottomless sky stands between us and the Fae forest. While we're on this side, no one can do anything to us."

Vidya nodded. "That's true, Willow. We're safe over here. But we still have the problem of the Fae magic fading."

"And what King Farrion said yesterday," reminded Lobey.

Vidya had not forgotten her father's words when Princess Sonakshi had woken him up for those brief few seconds.

'They're stealing the magic!'

"We still have to figure this out," said Vidya. She

stood up and went to Master Sunny's blackboard. She picked up a piece of chalk, feeling everyone's eyes on her.

"Alright," she said. "What do we know?" She drew dot points on the blackboard and spoke out loud. "We know that the Bunyips have woken up from their magical sleep and want revenge."

"We know that they have a King," said Lotus.

"And we know that *he* is stealing the Fae magic," said Lobey.

Vidya froze and turned around to look at the eldest triplet.

"Put two and two together, everyone," chided Lobey, thumping her hand against the table. "It has to be the Bunyips stealing the magic. This is no coincidence."

Vidya chewed on her lip. "I mean, it would make sense…" she said slowly.

"We have no real proof," said Willow.

"But how can we know for sure?" asked Lily.

It clicked together in Vidya's mind. There was no way around it.

"There's only one way to find out," she said. "It'll be difficult, but I think we need to do this."

"What do you mean?" asked Willow.

Vidya looked at Lily and her injured arm. "Lily, I know you're hurt, but you're our best tracker. Do you think you could track a Bunyip back to its King?"

Groans resounded around the table. Willow put his head in his hands, but Lotus' eyes shone with excitement, and Lobey bounced in her seat.

"Are you actually telling us we're going into the Bunyip's nest?" asked Willow into his hands. "These monsters that eat human men for breakfast? And we're going into their *nest*?"

"Yes," said Vidya firmly. "I won't force anyone to come with me. But we need to do this."

"I'm coming," said Lotus. "I want to get a better look at the things."

"Me too," grumbled Lily. "I don't like it, but I'll come, Vidya. I want to help. I can track them for sure."

"Oh, all right," said Willow unhappily. "I'm the best archer, anyway. I just hope I don't have to shoot any of them."

"Looks like the team is back then!" said Lotus, happily flexing his muscles. "When do we leave?"

* * *

At the crack of dawn the next morning, Vidya rolled out of bed, pulling Pancake with her. She splashed her face with cold water, patted it dry, and then washed Pancake's face for him too. She pulled on a green tunic and brown pants, colours that would blend in with the forest, she hoped.

She picked up *The Bunyip* book from her bedside table. It wasn't long, but it made it pretty clear that the Bunyips were dangerous, powerful creatures. She had seen that for herself in real life, after all. It made sense that her grandfather had needed to save the humans from them. And now, this very thing had come to bite them on the backside. She imagined if someone locked *her* up in a cave for hundreds of years, she would be furious once she woke up. The Bunyip King must be furious. But what revenge did he want? Her heart pumped unevenly in her chest. He would hate the Fae. He would want to come after them, and what? Take over the palace? Well, there was one thing keeping them safe, and as far as she saw it, there was no way the Bunyip King would be able to get past the Bottomless Sky. While they were in the palace, they were completely safe. That's the way it had been for thousands of years. The Fae were always protected.

But now, that was all going to change, because she was going to go and find the Bunyips. It would be dangerous and it risky, but if the adults falling asleep had told her anything, it was that she had to act to act fast. Somehow, the Bunyips were stealing Fae energy, and she needed to figure out how to get it back.

A heavy thought weighed at the back of her mind. If the Fae magic kept decreasing, the Fae children would end up falling asleep too. And then… it would be over. Everything would be over.

She went into her parents' room where Toad was sleeping on a mattress on the floor next to baby Mahiya's cot. They had lifted her father back onto the bed, and Vidya watched them all snoring softly in the dim not-yet morning light. *Give us some of your strength, mother*, she said in her mind. She had once witnessed her mother single-handedly take down a rogue crocodile that had gotten loose in the city. She smiled fondly at the memory of the all the Fae watching, open-mouthed, as their queen jumped on top of him and using rose bush vines, tied him up tight, transporting him back to the Fae pond he had come out of so the mermaids could take him back to the river where he lived.

Vidya tip-toed around the room, kissing them all on the forehead, including Toad, before shouldering her backpack and heading out the door.

* * *

She met the other three Fae kids in the entrance hall, eating bananas for energy. Lotus looked bright eyed and ready to go, yellow wings fluttering enthusiastically. Willow looked glum, but otherwise awake, gripping his bow tightly. Lily had a new bandage around her wrist but smiled at Vidya reassuringly. Vidya couldn't but help smile at the group. No matter how scary this mission was, these kids were still willing to do their part, and even be excited about it.

They walked out of the palace and rose into the air quickly in the same V formation from the Princess Sonakshi mission. They crossed the Bottomless Sky, and before they knew it; the team was in the trees of the Fae forest once again, the dawn sun colouring the sky pink.

Vidya's plan was simple. They would fly through the Fae forest and search for a Bunyip. Vidya had collected her father's strongest ghost berry juice. With it's help, they would follow the Bunyip back to their nest where they would hide in the trees and silently watch them, ready to gain any information about their new enemy.

They landed at the edge of the forest, Vidya handed out the ghostberry juice, and they all took a bottle each, draining it completely. They needed to be as ghostly as possible for as long as possible. Once Vidya collected the empty bottles back and they all looked like ghostly forms of themselves, they entered the forest on foot. Lily took the lead and fluttered up to a low branch on a gum tree. From there, she fluttered to the branch of the next tree. Lotus followed her pattern through the branches, with Vidya and Willow close behind. The Fae called this 'branch-hopping', and it was the easiest way to pass through a forest without being seen by a human, or in this case, Bunyip.

They fluttered from branch to branch deep into the forest where the trees grew closer to together and blocked out the sky completely. Vidya noticed, with unease, that the forest was quiet this morning. No birds chirped random words at them, nothing scurried beneath them. There was only silence.

Ahead, Vidya noticed Lily's ghostly body pause at one branch, Lotus stopping on the branch above her. Vidya paused on her own branch and felt Willow pause in the tree behind her. She strained her ears for any sign of danger. Lily fluttered down from her branch, and Vidya watched as she crouched to inspect the soil.

Above her, Lotus had his head cocked to one side, and his mouth was moving as if he were whispering. Willow fluttered next to Vidya and silently pointed to the branch above Lotus, where two red rosella birds were perched, looking down at Lotus and Lily. Within a minute, the rosellas flew away, and Lotus turned, beckoning them to fly to him. Vidya and Willow fluttered onto the branch next to him.

"Those birds were talking gibberish," he whispered. "The fading Fae magic is stopping them from talking normally, but I could tell they were warning me to get out. They kept saying 'danger'."

Vidya nodded sadly. Most the animals in the Kingdom were either sleeping or silent just like the adults.

Lily fluttered back up to them. "I can see the tracks down below," she whispered.

Vidya nodded, "Alright, let's go after it."

Lotus nodded and branch hopped to the next tree, the others following.

After a minute of hopping through the trees, they heard it. Heavy, dragging footsteps. Lotus stopped in his tracks again, and his body went rigid. He raised his hand up in the air. That was the signal that told them he was seeing a Bunyip. They all froze on their spots, listening and peering into the dark.

Lotus lowered his hand and turned, placing a finger to his lips. He waited a moment before carefully hopping onto the next branch. Vidya fluttered forward as silently as she could.

The Bunyip was walking just beyond their tree, its huge shiny black body moving slowly on powerful black legs. It's dog-like head was pointed at the ground, and it sort of swayed as if it were sleepy. It made its way through the forest, and silently, the four Fae children followed, fluttering through the branches. They were still in the Safe Zone of the forest, but none of them had ever been in this corner of it before.

It only took a few minutes before Lotus raised his hand again for them to all stop. Vidya could see a clearing up ahead, so there were no more branches for them to hop to. Lotus fluttered down to the ground, crouching behind a row of bushes, and signalled to the others to do the same.

All four of them crouched behind the bush, trying to peer through the leaves. Lotus pressed his finger to his lips again, his eyes wide. He pushed his hand through the bush and leaned back so Vidya could peer into the clearing.

Vidya had to cover her mouth to stop herself from gasping.

In that clearing, over one hundred Bunyips lay asleep. Hulking dark shapes made small black hills throughout the grass in front of a gigantic cavern. A huge boulder that must've sealed the entrance shut for all those years had been pushed to the side, leaving it wide open. The reality of the situation hit Vidya hard in the chest. This was the cave her grandfather had locked the Bunyips in two hundred years ago.

The strangest thing of all was the yellow glow coming out of the cave. It shone so warm and bright it was the complete opposite of everything that represented the Bunyips. Vidya felt as if the gold light was drawing her toward it, and she had the strongest urge to run into the cave and see where it was coming from. She did not realise she had leaned right forward until Willow gripped her arm strongly. Vidya shook herself when she realised she had been about to barge right through the bush into the clearing! She *needed* to see where that light was coming from, no doubt about it.

The four Fae children surveyed the Bunyips. This might be the only time they got to look at the creatures properly, without flying away in fear of being eaten. The beasts were huge to be sure; they had long powerful limbs and their faces were terrifying even during sleep, with drool dripping out of mouths full of sharp teeth. A few of them snored, rumbling softly throughout the clearing. But it was the sheer number of them that was overwhelming. Vidya noticed a chair in the centre of the clearing. It looked like it had been roughly put together, with a rock base and branches twined around to make the backrest. It looked like a throne. Then she saw a Bunyip, bigger than any other in the clearing, lay in front of it. His huge shape could have been mistaken for an enormous rock. *A throne,* Vidya thought. *A throne for a King.*

She shivered but was immediately drawn back to the cavern filled with that golden light. It was hard to ignore. Mesmerizing and intense, she was desperate to know more about it.

"What is that?" breathed Willow, nodding toward the cave with the golden light.

Vidya shook her head. "We need to find out." Something in her gut told her that this was it. This was important. But maybe a hundred Bunyips slept between them and the cave. How on earth would they get to see what was inside without waking a single one of them up?

Pancake squirmed in Vidya's pocket, and it was then Vidya had a spark of inspiration. She lifted Pancake out of her pocket. He looked at her with wide shining eyes.

"I need you to be brave for me, Pancake," she whispered. "Can you do that? For the Fae?"

Pancake gulped, but he nodded seriously.

"Okay, see that light over there? I need you to sneak in there and find out what it is."

Pancake's mouth fell open, but Vidya ignored him,

instead pulling out the spare bottle of ghostberry juice she had in her bag.

"Because you're so small, if you take this, you'll basically be invisible," she reassured him. "Just get in there and get out without waking anyone."

Pancake looked solemnly up at the four Fae who were staring at him and nodded.

She held the bottle of ghostberry juice and carefully tipped five drops into his mouth.

"Climb back up to my shoulder when you return."

Pancake nodded as his body disappeared. Vidya slowly lowered him to the ground and felt his weight shift off her palm as he scurried away.

Be careful, Pancake, she thought. She tried to steady her heart as it raced in her chest and focused on what was in front of her. She thought it might be smart to inspect the Bunyips while they were here, but she saw Lily had beaten her to it. In her hand was a pen and pad of paper, where she was quickly sketching out she shape of the Bunyip closest to them.

Vidya gazed at the cavern while they waited. That yellow glow was so familiar. Where had she seen it before? She'd known it from somewhere, she just knew it. Perhaps she needed to go to the library and see if she'd read about something like that before. Or maybe seen it. Maybe she had seen it in the Fae forest somewhere and forgotten about it? No, she decided, something like that she would never have forgotten about.

Just a few minutes later, Vidya felt a tiny movement by her shoe and then tiny claws up her leg. With a sigh of relief, she realised Pancake had come back and was climbing back up to her shoulder.

When he reached her shoulder, he began chattering excitedly non-stop in his quokka language, clearly very excited.

"Quiet, quiet!" hissed Lotus. "You'll give us away!"

"Quiet!" murmured Vidya, and Pancake stopped chattering. Instead, Vidya could hear him panting shakily on her shoulder, trembling with adrenaline. He would have to fill them in back at the castle. They couldn't afford any noise right now.

But it wasn't Pancake who gave them away.

The Bunyip closest to them rolled over in his sleep. As he did so, it revealed wide fleshy flaps attached to his back. Vidya's heart felt into her stomach.

Wings. They had somehow grown *wings.*

Vidya gasped loudly, and the Bunyip twitched and jerked upward, staring into the forest. Her reflexes took over, and she took a step backward, tripped on a rock she hadn't seen behind her, and fell with a loud. "Oof!"

Pancake shrieked as he fell off her shoulder.

Ten of the Bunyips closest to them jerked awake and jumped to their feet, growling deeply. This set off a reaction as the rest of the Bunyips in the clearing were awoken too. A Bunyip charged toward their hiding spot, growling. But he had not seen them yet.

"Go!" Lotus hissed.

Vidya scrambled to her feet, thrust Pancake in her pocket, and ran into the forest, flapping her wings quickly to get her into the air. She felt the other three close behind her as Bunyips, Vidya could not tell how many, thrashed into the bushes after them.

"Fae!" came a deep grumbling roar.

"They can speak!" shrieked Willow. "Up! Up! Up!"

Vidya had reached one branch of a tall tree and flapped her wings again to get her up to the next branch.

The four Fae branched hopped upward, and a second later, Vidya heard Lotus cry out.

"Urgh!" Vidya stopped in her tracks to look down and see one Bunyip had made it up one branch and had Lotus' ankle in one huge black claw.

Other Bunyips were trying to fly upward to catch them, but as they jumped and flapped their wings, they clumsily gained a small height but then came tumbling down.

Above her, Vidya heard the *twang* of Willow's bow string. With a roar, the Bunyip holding Lotus fell away, clutching his shoulder where an arrow was now buried.

Lotus was released with a shout of surprise, and as the Bunyip crashed to the ground, the four Fae kids flew upward, quickly gaining height into the treetops.

"They can't fly properly," wheezed Lotus. "Did you see? They can't use their wings properly yet."

Finally, they reached the topmost branches of the dense trees, where they could see the blue sky peeking through the gaps. The four kids burst through the canopy, into the open sky. They gratefully breathed in the crisp morning air. They were free, and in the safety of the sky once again.

But for how long? Vidya thought as they flew as fast as they could away from the Bunyip nest. How long will the skies remain free and safe for us? Somehow, the Bunyips had developed wings. They were no longer as safe in their sky palace as they had thought.

9

UNDER THE SEA

The most ancient friends of the Fae are the people of the water, the Merfolk. The custodians of the Sea were born of the water before anything else. But as the sea is beautiful and wise, wild and unforgiving, so are its children.

—The Book of the Fae, Queen Mab the First, 3333 B.C.

Willow, Lotus, Lily, and the triplets had all taken up residence in Vidya's room. Luna and Toad were spreading tea tree lotion over Lotus' sore ankle where the Bunyip had gotten a hold of him. The rest of them were eating Daisy's broccoli stew or dozing on the bed or on small mattresses they had laid on the floor. Lobey was sleeping on the window seat, leafing through one of the books on Bunyips. The new information about the Bunyip's wings had shaken them, and, exhausted from their trek into the forest and then chase back home, they collapsed into Vidya's room while Vidya told the triplets what had happened. The triplets had responded with pale faces and shocked expressions. *"Rest,"* Lobey had said, pulling at her blue braid, *"and then we will decide what to do."*

But Vidya could not sleep like Lily and Willow immediately had. She reclined against her fluffy green pillows, chewing her lip as Pancake sat next to her with a paper and pen in hand. He had been excited to tell her all about what he had seen in the glowing cave, but his quokka squeaks made no sense to her. In the end, she had given him drawing tools so he could show her. She watched as he sketched out a rough shape. Lotus drew up a chair to watch, and Luna and Toad came to stand behind him.

"It looks like…" Lotus squinted at the rounded shape. "A rock?"

"It's the flower," breathed Vidya, watching as Pancake added definition to the petals. "Is that what it is, Pancake?"

Pancake nodded vigorously, then took a yellow pencil and started adding colour to the petals, then adding streaks of light coming out of it. Vidya remembered the mystical glow from the cave. It was as if it had been drawing her in. *Come in,* the light said. *Vidya, come closer*. She rubbed the goosebumps that erupted all over the arms.

"It's a yellow flower," said Luna, cocking her head.

Pancake shook his head and held up the yellow pencil and sighed. He cast his eye about the room, peering around. Then he saw something on the Fae

EKTAA BALI

wall and squeaked excitedly, jumping off the bed and around Lotus to rush to the other side of the room. He climbed up onto Vidya's desk and held up a golden earring.

"It's gold?" Vidya asked in disbelief.

"What kind of flower is gold?" asked Lobey with disbelief. "None—"

"There is one," interrupted Vidya in a soft voice. Everyone went quiet and stared at her. Something in her spine tingled, and she knew she was on the right path. "It sounds crazy, but all know the one flower that is gold."

"No," breathed Luna.

"Don't be ridiculous," snorted Lobey. "The Flower of Awakening is a myth. A legend. It's just a story they tell kids."

"Yes," said Vidya seriously. "*The* story, about how we got our magic. About how we came from the earth."

"If the Flower of Awakening actually existed," droned Lobey, unimpressed. "Our people would've found it by now. There's not a single living plant we don't know about."

Vidya thought back to the cave. That glow was so strong, so beautiful, so wonderful, it almost didn't seem real. She looked at Lotus, and he looked back at her. She could see it in his eyes, he were thinking the same thing she was thinking, remembering the beauty of the glow.

"You didn't see it, Lobelia," said Lotus, turning in his chair to speak to her. "It's like nothing else I've ever seen. I'll never forget it."

Lobey sighed. "Maybe it was another type of flower? I can't tell much by Pancake's drawing."

"We'll have a look in the library," said Luna. "Maybe there are pictures in a book somewhere?"

"Good thinking, Luna," said Vidya. "I can't just lie here, I'm going to head down there right now."

She didn't have to explain her urgency to the others. They had seen the wings on the Bunyips. And just because they couldn't fly now, didn't mean they wouldn't learn quickly. How long would they be safe in the palace? Vidya knew she had to work quickly. They needed answers. They needed to be sure. They needed a plan.

Vidya jumped out of bed and scooped Pancake up.

"I'll come too," said Lobey.

"I'll go and check on baby Mahiya," said Toad. "It must be time to change her again soon."

Vidya thanked Toad, and left the others to rest, shoving Pancake in her pocket and sweeping out of the room and down the stairs to the library, Lobey close on her heels. They were just passing the entrance hall, when she felt a magical wind whip through the front door. A green leaf tumbled through the entrance, and Vidya leapt toward it, snatching it out of the air.

The leaf was slightly wet, so it took her a second to make out the inky words.

Emergency. Meet me at the Fae pond today, when your sun is highest ~ Meera.

. . .

It was Princess Meera! Bob must have taken the leaf to her, and now she had information to share.

When your sun is highest. The sun was highest at noon. Vidya looked out the large front windows. The sun was high in the sky, but not quite at its peak. She might just have enough time to get there.

Vidya showed Lobey the message.

"I told Bob, Meera's assistant, to send me a message when she had information for us. She knows something. The day we took Princess Sonakshi back to the portal, Bob told us she had information. I have to go now."

Lobey took all of this in with a frown on her face.

"Vidya, just wait a minute—"

"We don't have time, Lobey!" Vidya urged. *"I have to go now."*

Vidya could see the gears turning behind Lobey's eyes.

"Who are you taking?" she asked.

Vidya shook her head, "They've been through enough for today. Let them sleep, I'll go alone."

"That's stupid, Vidya. Let me come."

"I need you to look after things here, Lobey," said Vidya, rubbing her eyes. "You're next in line to the throne after me. You know that as well as I do."

That made Lobey shut her mouth. She screwed up her eyes and shook her head. "I would make a great Queen you know," she said fiercely.

Vidya turned toward the entrance to the palace, waving her hands at Lobey. "Yeah, yeah, I know. If I'm not back by dark, send a search party in the morning."

. . .

Vidya ran down the rest of the path and shot over the Bottomless Sky, fluttering her wings as fast as she ever had and landed with a thump on the other side.

She strode into the tree line of the forest and peered through the trees. Thankfully, there was no unusual movement in the shadows between the trees. No Bunyips yet.

The Fae forest felt like a huge dark shadow at her back. She had never actually been here by herself. She had always come with one of the other guards, or even her father. Her heart ached as she realised she missed him so much right now and wondered what his first move would be when he returned. Would he take a group of Fae into the forest and round up the Bunyips like Grandfather Fern had? But the Bunyips were smarter now, Vidya didn't think he'd be able to do it the same way. The Old Ones must've given him some wisdom or knowledge that would give them the answer. Perhaps they would know about the Flower of Awakening, or whatever that golden glow was. She trusted Pancake to be honest, of course, but he was only a young quokka and new to the ways of the Fae world. Maybe he thought he saw a flower, and it was actually something else.

Vidya turned and looked into the shadows of the forest. If she was quiet, a Bunyip should not catch her getting to the Fae pond. She branch-hopped through the trees easily. The forest was empty except for a few birds fast asleep in nests safely high in the trees. But of course they did not make any noise, making the forest eerily quiet. She could only hear the flutter of her own wings, the creak of the branches under her weight as she landed, and sometimes a breeze rustling the leaves.

She arrived at the Fae pond quickly and she scoped the clearing that surrounded it. There were no animals or Bunyips in sight. There was the glowing blue pool of water and the rocks bordering it, but the water was clear, and Bob was now where to be seen. It was just past midday, Princess Meera should be here by now.

As she was watching the pond nervously, a shadow appeared under the surface. A grey shape jumped out of the pond, made a wide arc and then splashed back into the water.

"Bob!" Vidya whispered to herself. *He must be checking if I've arrived*.

Vidya looked left and right, there were still no Bunyips in sight, and fluttered down right near the pond. She leaned over the pond and stuck her hand into it, waving it around beneath the surface.

Two shadows appeared this time, rapidly growing larger, and this time, gloomy faced Bob was not alone.

"Good afternoon," came the rough voice of the girl who was, no doubt about it—Princess Meera.

She was paler than Vidya, for surely she did not get much sun, with skin the colour of milk tea, and wide blue eyes the same colour as the water of the Fae pond. She wore a crop top made of shiny seashells and had long, wavy black hair. Over her shoulder, Vidya could see the hilt of a sword strapped to her back. The hilt was made of coral and sapphire and gleamed in the sunlight that streamed through the canopy of the trees.

"Hello, I'm Princess Vidya," Vidya held out her hand.

"Oh, well met, I'm Princess Meera," she shook Vidya's hand.

"Hello again, Bob," said Vidya, to which the grumpy fish bobbed his head up and down in the water.

"Now," said Meera briskly. "I've found something you need to see. It was guarded by a terrible monster, but I dealt with her. It's a haunting tale of daring and valour and perhaps one day I will tell it to you, but right now, we must hurry." She lifted a finger and pointed it down toward the water she was floating in. "The Fae ponds are misfiring on your side. The Fae magic that powers them is fading."

Vidya stared at the Fae pond with a sinking feeling in her chest. First the adults fall asleep and now the Fae ponds were faulty? However the Bunyips were stealing their magic, they needed to fix it fast.

"How do we do this?" Vidya asked. "I can't swim underwater for long."

"I've come prepared," said Meera. "The Fae used to use a water bubble to visit with the merpeople." She moved back in the Fae pond, and Bob followed her. From under the water, she brought out a large lily pad. It was a broad, green, circular leaf, big enough that Vidya could stand on it. Meera spread it out on top of the water so it floated on the surface. "Alright, hop on top!"

"I'll sink straight down! And Pancake can't swim!"

"Who's Pancake?" asked Meera, raising her eyebrows.

Pancake squeaked, coming out of Vidya's pocket and scrambling up to her shoulder. He pointed at the lily pad and squeaked in dismay.

"What is he?" asked Meera, peering at him.

"He's a quokka," Vidya answered fondly.

"Well, you're a happy fellow, aren't you?" said Meera, amused. "Take these." Vidya held her hand out as Meera dropped two tiny conch shells into her hand. "Put them in your ears, that way I can talk to you in the water." Meera fit two tiny shells into her ears too. "Anyway, I don't have time to explain, but yes, you and Pancake will be able to breathe underwater. Hop on, and you'll see. Bob said this place is full of Bunyips."

Remembering that this was indeed true, Vidya shrugged to herself and stepped right onto the lily pad before she could think about it any more. But the lily pad did not crumple and fold underneath her weight as she had initially thought. Instead, it felt as firm as if she stood on land.

"Let's go!" Meera, and she dipped beneath the water, her purple-green tail visible for a moment before it disappeared beneath the surface, while Bob stayed to watch Vidya. Immediately, the lily pad began to submerge itself beneath the water, lowering Vidya slowly down like an elevator.

"Argh!" Vidya exclaimed.

"Keep still," droned Bob. "Look at your feet."

Vidya looked down, and instead of water surrounding her feet, they stayed dry—no water spilled onto the lily pad at all. As it sunk into the water, a silvery wall appeared at the edges, stopping water from flowing in. Pancake and Vidya watched in fascination as the lily pad then lowered into the water while the water was kept back by the silvery bubble. Soon, they were deep enough that Vidya could see into the water beyond the silver bubble. She and Pancake looked upward just as the silvery bubble closed in on them, and they were completely in, water on all sides of them, and it looked like they were in an underwater cave, the Fae pond making a little hole in the top of it. Meera was waiting for her just beyond in the cave, her dark hair floating around her. She grinned and waved. Vidya waved back and watched as Bob, looking very unimpressed, kept still while Meera tied a rope around him like a horse's harness and bridle. Meera led him to Vidya's bubble, and with the two long ends, tied them to Vidya's lily pad.

"I call it a Bubblepad", came Meera's voice in Vidya's ear.

Vidya jumped because Meera had not moved her mouth at all, but the sound was still coming from the conch shell earpiece.

"It's weird, I know, came Meera's voice again. *But under the water, merfolk either use sign language or talk to each other telepathically. Which means I can talk to you through your mind. Using the earpiece, you can talk to me too."*

Bob swished his tail in irritation, and Vidya saw that he was hitched up to her bubble so that he could pull her through the water.

"Bob is a bit annoyed". Meera's voice came again. *"Usually, I use our seahorses to pull a Bubblepad, but I don't want my mother knowing what I've been up to just yet. I'll probably get in trouble."*

Meera rolled her eyes as if very annoyed by this.

Vidya raised her eyebrows. "Where are we going exactly?" she asked nervously. "What did you find?"

"I think it's best I just show you," said Meera. *"Let's go, we have a long way to go."* She turned and swam down and forward, Vidya squinted to try and see her through the darkness of the cave.

Bob swam forward, and Vidya rocked on her 'Bubblepad' as they began to move through the dark water.

"Here we go, Pancake," said Vidya, as the Quokka clung onto her shoulder, watching around in awe. "We're in a new world now. I bet you're the first quokka to go under the sea like this!"

Pancake nodded proudly.

Vidya sat down, crossed legged on the Bubblepad, and Pancake settled on her lap for the ride.

She took some Bilberry essence from her bag and gulped it down, then gave some to Pancake.

"This is why Willow's eyes are so sharp. Billberry helps us see better in the dark," she explained to him. "There's not much light down here."

The bilberry sharpened their eyes so they could make out the shapes in the dark ocean.

"Oh, sorry," came Meera's voice in Vidya's ear. *"I've forgotten that merpeople can practically see in the dark."*

"It's okay," said Vidya. "Are we travelling through an underwater cave?"

"*Yes*," said Meera.

As the bilberry juice kicked in, Vidya could just make out the shadow of tail ahead. It was an eerie thing to be moving through an underwater cave through the dark like this.

"*Just up ahead,*" continued Meera. "*There is some glowing seaweed I use sometimes. Oh, here!*"

They must have entered a section of the caves where it opened up suddenly because they were all at once surrounded by a cave full of swaying seaweed that glowed green and purple.

"*Now you'll be able to see me!*" Meera said, happily waving at them. She had tied a bunch of the glowing green seaweed and placed it like a headband on her head and used another length to circle the lower part of her tail.

"That's brilliant," smiled Vidya. "Thank you."

"*Alright, Bob,*" Meera nodded. "*Let's make it snappy. This part of the cave is...*" her voice trailed off.

"What was that?" asked Vidya nervously.

"Oh nothing, nothing," waved Meera, swimming ahead. Bob pulled them forward, and they moved into a dark corridor once again. The only thing in the mass of black water was the glowing seaweed on Meera's tail.

By the way they moved through the water, Vidya could tell that somehow, Bob pulled them through the water at a rapid pace, and she vaguely wondered what on earth the little fish ate to give him so much energy. On and on they travelled through the darkness, with Bob swerving left and right through the maze of the cave system, following Meera's lead. Meera had clearly been down here before, and Vidya wondered how the mermaid princess travelled around this place alone without being scared.

Before long, Meera's voice came again.

"Hey you! Out of the way!"

Vidya jumped, but she realised Meera was not talking to her. Bob paused in the water, Vidya and Pancake strained to see through the water, but it looked like Meera had turned a corner.

"I'm Princess Meera, you fool, submit to me or submit to my sword! Out. Of. My. Way."

"Meera, what's going on?" asked Vidya nervously.

There was the sound of a grunt, and then—*"Oh, it's fine, Vidya, I dealt with him. Bob come on."*

Bob turned the corner, and they passed Meera floating to one side, her sword drawn. She waved them forward. *"The exit is just there, Bob, go on. I want to make sure we're not followed. These idiots think they can outsmart me..."*

Vidya and Pancake exchanged a look as Meera waved her sword angrily through the water as they passed. Bob pulled them forward and suddenly, the darkness opened up to wide blue water. They were down by the sea floor, and looking up, they were so far down, Vidya couldn't make out the surface. A couple of fish swam past her, and Pancake squeaked excitedly.

"Let's go!" Meera rushed forward, moving her tail powerfully, and Bob had to hurry to catch up.

They watched their surroundings as Bob swept them past coral, rock, and seaweed.

Soon, the seafloor became rocky, and as they travelled, the rocks grew bigger and became boulders. Then the boulders grew bigger and became rocky hills. Then the rocky hills became mountains of rock, soaring high above them.

"The world in the ocean is much the same as the world above it", Meera said as she swam. *"We have mountains here too."*

"I never knew," said Vidya in amazement, craning her neck to look at how high they went. They were really far below the surface. Then a thought struck her.

"How much air is in the Bubblepad?" she asked.

Meera glanced back. *"It should be just enough. When the air runs out, the bubble pops open. Oh! We're almost there."*

Vidya could not help but notice that this part of the ocean was strangely quiet. It had the same sort of sinister lack of life that the Fae forest had just this morning. The type of quiet that meant there was something dangerous nearby. She clutched onto Pancake firmly and surveyed the dark blue water around her. She wondered how much protection the silver Bubblepad would give her if a shark or unfriendly sea creature tried to get at them.

Meera came to a stop in front of them. She pointed to a towering mountain.

In the rock was a gigantic, gaping hole. A black mouth in which Vidya could not see inside.

"Are we going in there?" Vidya asked, looking side to side.

"Unfortunately, yes", Meera unsheathed her sword again. *"Bob, stick close."*

Bob pulled them inside the cave, and Vidya cringed internally. But her first view of a threatening sea monster was not as she had expected.

A giant creature lay on the cave sea floor. It was leathery and rough, with long tentacles and half covered in sand. It wasn't moving or breathing.

"Did you kill this creature?" asked Vidya, wide eyed.

"No", Said Meera. *"I killed that one."*

As they passed the creature, the head of a gigantic shark became visible.

"Creatures gravitate toward this place. When one dies, another comes to replace it."

"Who killed the other one?" asked Vidya.

Meera remained silent and continued to swim forward. They turned a corner, and Vidya's heart jumped when she saw a familiar golden light pouring out of an opening in the rock.

It felt and looked exactly like the light from the Bunyip cave, just a bit softer.

Meera led them into the gap in the rock, and Vidya could see the golden glow came from the cavern floor. Vidya squinted at the floor to get a better look and found the source of the glow were tiny objects scattered about the sand.

"They're petals", said Meera. She beckoned Bob to bring the Bubblepad closer. *"Look",* Meera pointed in the centre of the cavern.

A large dent was in the sandy-soil, as if it had been newly dug up and something had been removed.

"The petals," Vidya whispered.

"Petals from a golden flower that glows with its own light", said Meera. *"A flower that no one knew was here. That was heavily guarded by fierce creatures since the dawn of time."*

"No one believed me," whispered Vidya. "I told them, but no one believed me."

Meera turned her blue eyes to gaze at Vidya with seriousness.

Vidya felt it in her bones. These petals… they called out to her. She knew, she just knew what it was.

Meera picked up a petal and held it up to the silvery bubble and pushed it through. The bubble bent, then admitted Meera's hand with the petal whist not letting any water in.

Pancake reached out and took it from her, Meera pulled her hand back out.

"Flower of Awakening," Pancake whispered.

Vidya almost jumped ten feet in the air.

"Pancake, did you just speak?" she asked, shocked.

Pancake looked at Vidya, then looked at the petal he was holding and dropped it, covering his mouth with his claw.

"Wow!" came his muffled voice.

Realisation dawned on Vidya.

"This is how they're smart. This is how they grew wings! It changes creatures," breathed Vidya, looking at Meera with wide eyes. "They've found it." Her knees felt weak, she thought she was going to be sick. "They've taken it."

Meera came toward them right up to her bubble. "You've seen it?"

"I saw it," Pancake raised his hand. "Same petal."

Meera shook her head. "And it's not they. It's Him."

"Who?" asked Vidya, frowning.

"The kraken lying out there in the entrance told me before he died. The creature that took it called himself the Bunyip King."

Vidya swallowed a couple of times. Her mouth felt incredibly dry. Things just kept getting worse and worse. Pancake reached up and patted her cheek.

"Answers, we have now," he whispered.

"We have answers now," she corrected him absentmindedly, gazing at the golden petal on the floor of the bubble pad with wonder. She bent to pick it up, feeling its softness in her hands. A warm, fuzzy feeling spread over her chest, and she couldn't but help smile at the petal. *Tired*, it seemed to say. *So tired*. And a flash in her mind's eye made her lose her breath. The image of a magnificent golden flower, like nothing she had ever seen before, appeared to her. Golden, glowing, ancient and spectacular. *Help me, Vidya*, came an ethereal, whispering voice. She gasped.

"Is it saying something?" came Meera's voice.

Vidya's head jerked up in surprise, the image fading away, and Meera's pale face peered at her. She had forgotten where she was for a minute. "What did you say?"

"You were looking at it like it was saying something. Fae talk to plants, don't they?"

Vidya shook her head. "No, only our guardian plant."

"What's a guardian plant?"

"All Fae are born with one plant they can talk to specially. We become keepers of that species of plant. Look after it, and it gives us powers back."

"Oh, so what's yours?"

Vidya looked back down at the golden petal and frowned deeply, then shook her head. "I—um, don't know yet."

"Oh. Could it be this flower?"

Vidya immediately shook her head as a reflex. That was impossible. Why would *she* have *the* Flower of Awakening as her guardian plant? The thought was ridiculous. But, she thought, just yesterday, the thought of the flower even being real was ridiculous. Had she heard the petal speak to her? Or did she just make it up in her head? Maybe the flower spoke to everyone?

"I don't know."

"Well, we should get out of here," said Meera. *"This is one of the most dangerous parts of the ocean."*

Vidya nodded, and Meera pushed through a couple more petals for Pancake to collect. Chances were, they might be useful, and Vidya knew she could never come back here again.

Meera led them out of the cave, and Bob followed with Vidya and Pancake deep in thought.

The Flower of Awakening was real, she had evidence. The others would have to believe her now. But being real made their situation all the worse. The Bunyip King had their prized possession in his keeping, and it was clearly giving him power. The thought of him hurting it was an awful thought, more than Vidya could bear. He just couldn't hurt it, he just couldn't!

No, thought Vidya, he's not hurting it. They're using it. That must be how they had gotten their wings, and their smarts, no doubt about it. The Flower sang and had awoken the Fae from the earth. It was capable of incredible magic. Who knows what it could do?

"Let's get out of here", came Meera's voice. *"We should get you back."*

As they began their journey away from the underwater mountains and back the way they had come, Vidya felt the back of her neck prickle. How long had they been under the ocean? It felt like hours, definitely. Crossing her fingers, she hoped it was still daylight by the time they made it back. She willed Bob to swim faster, but the fish was only a little guy, and it was clearly taking a toll on him to be pulling both her and Pancake through the water for so long.

"It must be late, Pancake," she said.

He nodded his head in agreement.

After what seemed like forever, they entered the familiar cave where the Fae pond was located. Meera slowed down ahead of them, and as Vidya looked upward, she saw the small dark circle that was the Fae pond.

Oh no, she thought, seeing that there was no light coming through the patch. It was definitely night.

She watched as Meera swam right up to the Fae

pond entrance and knocked her head right into it as if it were made of solid glass.

"*Ow!*" she cried, rubbing her head.

"What's wrong?" asked Vidya, panicked.

Meera swam back up to the glassy surface and tapped it with her finger. "The Fae pond is shut. It won't let me through."

Vidya's heart froze in her chest. "How can it do that? I don't think I have much air left in here."

Meera put her hands on her lips and looked around them. *"We could find another Fae pond, I guess..."*

To Vidya's horror, the silvery bubble faded around them. She shouted a warning just as water flooded around them on all sides.

"Don't panic!" came Meera's shout in her ear.

Vidya flailed in the water, kicking her legs so she didn't sink. She grabbed Pancake, who was flapping his arms and legs around in terror.

"Maybe we can break it!" Cried Meera.

Vidya and Meera swam up to the glassy underside of the Fae pond and pounded their fists against it, but it felt like solid ice against their skin. Vidya's lungs burned, heart pounding fast. She needed air. Badly.

But she was stuck, and there was no way out.

Pancake released the air he was holding in a cloud of bubbles. Then he went limp.

10

THE FAE QUEEN

In the home of the Old Ones, one speaks with a voice leaden with the reverence of he who knows he was about to receive information of utmost import. In the home of the Old Ones, one sees with eyes that glisten from the sight of something granted only to them. In the home of the Old Ones, one treads with feet heavy with the weight of what brought them there.

—The Book of the Fae, Queen Mab the First, 3333 B.C.

Vidya clutched Pancake to her chest. She could feel her heart pounding in her ears, her throat burned, she wanted to breathe so badly.

"Hold on, Vidya, please!" Came Meera's cry from the conch shell earpiece in her ear. Meera was thrashing around in the water, fists banging again and again on the glassy underside of the Fae pond.

"Let us in!" She cried.

In an explosion of white bubbles, something long and hard burst through the portal above them. A barky arm grabbed Vidya around the waist, and she was pulled upward through the water.

Cold night air stung her face, and she gasped and spluttered, water streaming out from her nose as something thumped her on the back.

"Oh, for Earth's sake, Vidya!" cried a familiar, rude voice.

"L-lobey?" asked Vidya, as something released her onto the ground. She rubbed at her eyes to make out the dark shapes in the clearing.

"Yes, it's me, you crazy Fae," Lobey said angrily, a little further away. "Oh wake up Pancake!"

Vidya scrambled to her feet as her vision cleared. On the other side of the pond stood a tall Devil's Finger Tree, swaying softly, and beneath it, Lobey was on her knees over the soggy round of fur that was Pancake. As Vidya watched in shock, Princess Meera leapt out of the water and came to sit on the side of the Fae pond. She leaned over, pinched Pancake's nose, and blew into his mouth. The little quokka reacted immediately, coughing, water pouring from his mouth. But that wasn't all that came out. A golden, glowing petal of from the Flower of Awakening stuck out of Pancake's mouth, and Meera exclaimed. She pulled it out with her fingers as Pancake wheezed.

Once it was out, Lobey rolled him on his side, whacking him on the back.

"You're alright," cooed Meera, placing the petal on a

rock. "That was a close one," she said, looking up at Lobey. "What is that?" she asked, pointing at the Devil's Finger.

"That," said Lobey with her nose in the air. "Is my guardian plant. This one I call Jimmy."

Vidya gaped at the Devil's Finger tree, standing calmly at Lobey's back, then at Lobey's brown face. Lobey nodded knowingly. "I know," she said quietly as Pancake scrambled over the rocks to Vidya. She picked him up and squeezed him, trying to wring the water out of his coat.

"That's sure something," said Vidya. "Thanks, Lobey, without your help, we were goners."

"I know," she said curtly, patting Jim's rough bark. The tree leaned into her hand like a puppy wanting a scratch. "Luna told me that a couple of the kids out in the city said they had seen a Fae pond freeze over, like it was a human pond in winter! I knew you'd be in trouble then. I flew over here and tried to break it open with a stick, but it wouldn't work. Then this guy showed up."

She patted Jimmy fondly. "And I could *hear* him, Vidya, like actually hear his voice in my head. *What's the problem*? He asked, and I said, 'I need to get through this thing.' Then I saw you three hovering like shadows underneath. I saw Meera's fist, and then Jimmy broke through."

"Well, thanks, Jimmy," said Vidya gratefully. "What a time to find out your guardian plant, hey?"

Lobey shook her head. "I had a suspicion when we

went to find Nani in the greenhouse, but I wasn't sure. We didn't spend long in there."

Meera held up the sodden golden petal. "You guys will have a lot to discuss."

"Did that come out of Pancake's tummy?" asked Lobey, recoiling in disgust.

"No," said Vidya, leaning over the Fae pond to take the petal. "Lobey, this is a petal from the Flower of Awakening."

Lobey's mouth hung open.

"All this time," explained Vidya. "It was being guarded under the sea."

"It's true," said Meera glumly. "I was the one who found it missing. There's a big old hole in the sand down there."

"The Bunyip King has it now," said Vidya. "It changes animals, look—" She held up Pancake.

"Hi Lobey," he squeaked.

Lobey almost fell over. "Animals take years to learn English from the Fae!"

"Yep," said Vidya, cuddling a shivering Pancake to her once more. "But holding the petal made Pancake speak straight away. That must be how the Bunyips can think and grew their wings."

"The Flower of Awakening brought us up from the soil and made us guardians of the Earth. It makes sense that it has incredible powers to change creatures like that," said Lobey.

Vidya nodded. But what more could it do?

"You'd better get out of here," said Meera, peering

around at the dark clearing. "It's not wise to be out here at night time."

"And we're freezing," shivered Pancake. Vidya smiled at him despite her own freezing bones. His cute little voice would never get old.

"Thanks, Princess Meera," said Vidya. "Without you, we might not have been able to figure this out."

Meera brushed her fingers through her long black hair and smiled. "I'm not sure when I'll see you again if the Fae ponds are not working," she gestured at the glassy shards of the Fae pond in front of her. The surface had already begun to reform, staring to close it off once again. "I wish I could've helped you more. But it looks like you guys are fighting this war on your own."

Vidya and Lobey exchanged a worried look.

"We'll be okay," said Vidya hopefully. "Especially now we have the Devil's Fingers on our side."

They bade goodbye to Meera, who jumped back into her Fae pond to join Bob, her purple tail rapidly disappearing below the water.

"Jimmy will escort us back to the cliff," said Lobey, leading them out of the clearing. "He lives deep in the forest here with his family, so he can come back if I call for him."

But they had only been walking for a minute before an almighty roar made the ground beneath them tremble. Vidya and Lobey's heads snapped toward one another, mirroring the others' terrified look. But that roar was joined by another, and another again. The colour drained from Lobey's face, and Pancake shook violently in Vidya's arms.

"Run!" hissed Lobey.

"No!" Vidya grabbed the girl's sleeve. "Fly!"

The girls leapt up into the air, fluttering their wings, but Vidya had forgotten that her magenta wings were still damp from the water. So as Lobey ascended up into the trees, Vidya tumbled back down to the ground. Jimmy scooped her up just as Lobey let out an ear shattering scream.

Two Bunyips crashed through the trees, their dark forms like black menacing demons towering above her. One swiped at Vidya. Jimmy swept her out of harm's way with one of his powerful branch-arms. But the second Bunyip roared and came at Jimmy with his mouth wide open and with a loud crunch, broke into Jimmy's trunk.

"Grab Fae!" came a gravelly voice. "Get them!" came the voice of another.

Vidya's heart pounded in her chest. This was the second time she had heard them speak. Up close, their voices were terrifying, and also intelligent. These were not stupid creatures at all.

Lobey screamed Jimmy's name from the trees. And a third Bunyip crashed into the scene. But this one leapt up into the air and, with a powerful sweep of his fleshy wings, flew right into the trees.

"Go, Lobey!" cried Vidya, "Fly away!"

The other two Bunyips flapped their wings uselessly. It seemed they hadn't gotten the hang of flying yet. Jimmy grabbed Vidya around the waist as Pancake screamed from inside her pocket, bolting away from the Bunyips as fast as his roots could carry him. Jimmy was fast, and he seemed to be able to see through the forest in the dark, instinctively knowing which rocks and roots to avoid. The Bunyips crashed through the trees behind them, and Vidya's mind raced, trying to see a way out of this. Her wings were drying, but they still felt damp. She couldn't fly her way out of this just yet. The other problem was, she couldn't tell which way Jimmy was taking her, his rooty-feet were pounding away into the forest, and it felt to Vidya as if he were leading the Bunyips deeper into the forest, not toward the cliff edge by the Palace.

"J-j-jimmy!" she cried, but it was impossible to talk as he jostled her with each stride of his legs, carrying Vidya like a rag doll through the Fae forest. On and on he ran, and quite quickly, the sounds of the running Bunyips behind them got fainter and fainter, but Jimmy did not slow down. He seemed so spooked by the Bunyip that had bitten part of his trunk off that he wasn't going to stop until he probably felt safe, which was likely when he got back to his home.

Stop, Jimmy Vidya silently urged him *Oh Earth, help us! Stop, Jimmy, Stop! Please.*

Vidya could feel the forest around her close in the way her father had described the deepest parts of the Fae forest. The trees grew tall and wide and menacing. It was so dark and damp that the very air got heavy and made it difficult to breathe. Vidya couldn't take it anymore. She was so tired, she just needed him to stop. She beat on the branch arms that held her tight.

"L-let me go, Jimmy!" she cried weakly. She punched at his arms. Pancake, likely inspired by Vidya's efforts, opened his mouth and bit down hard on Jimmy's barky arm.

Jimmy, surprised by his second bite of the night and traumatised already by the sensation of teeth on his bark, stumbled upon his own roots. Vidya felt him release his grip around her waist and as he tripped and fell, she flew through the air, her wings flailing uselessly behind her, Pancake cried out as he too soared through the air. The two of them hit an impossibly enormous tree and slumped onto the soft soil. Jimmy, terrified enough for the night, didn't notice he had lost Vidya and got onto the root-feet once again and continued his run back to his family of trees, deeper into the forest.

But neither Jimmy nor Vidya had been in the right state of mind as they had run through the Fae forest. Unknowingly, Jimmy had run east. Unknowingly, Vidya, the current leader of the Eastern Bushland Kingdom, had called out for help. And unknowingly, they had run straight into the middle of the Old Country.

When Vidya and Pancake woke up, sunlight streamed through the trees—impossibly huge trees as big and as tall as mountains. She stood, rubbing her eyes, staring up at the impossibly blue sky she could see through the bright evergreen leaves. A sweet wind tickled her cheek, and as she cast her eye around her, her heart skipped a beat in her chest. She knew she was not in the Fae forest anymore.

"Pancake," she whispered. The little quokka's mouth was hanging open as he stared at their surroundings. "I think... I think..." but she couldn't say it out loud, so she scooped him and held him close to her, because she needed to feel like something was real and sure. That this wasn't all a dream that she didn't understand. Together, they walked through the Old Country, smelling the sweet air, craning their necks at the tallest trees she had ever seen. It felt like her eyes weren't big enough to take it all in. She wondered if her father felt the same when he came here himself, only a few days ago. She just walked in the direction that felt right, where it felt good to her, and eventually, the trees stopped, forming a ring around a huge grassy plain. It was a clearing. Just as her father had once described to her. *The* clearing. A smooth flat rock sat just in front of her, out past the line of trees. She gazed at it for a moment, wondering what to do next. And then Pancake took out the now dry golden petal and held it up to her. Her mouth made a tiny 'oh', and she nodded. Her father had taught her the old ways of things. She took the golden petal with its faded glow and stepped forward to place it gently on the stone.

"A petal," she whispered. "From the Flower of Awakening. This is my offering."

A gentle breeze rustled the leaves on the trees behind her, but nothing happened.

"Old ones," Vidya whispered. "Princess Vidya of the Eastern Bushland Fae requests your help." She closed her eyes and waited.

It began as a rumble in the distance, and Vidya's heart almost leapt out of her chest.

Boom, boom, boom, the steady, heavy beat sounded all around her. The ground beneath her vibrated with each thump, and Vidya realised they were the sound of impossibly heavy footsteps.

And then they entered the clearing, and both Vidya and Pancake had to remind themselves to breathe. Vidya remembered them all from Master Sunny's classes many years ago. The Old Ones were an important part of their history, and everyone knew who they were.

The Great Echidna arrived first, bumbling in on all fours, but unlike tiny Uncle Jula-wil, she was enormous, with spines twice the length of any man's arm.

The Great Platypus stood next to her, as big as a cow.

The Great Marsupial Lion was three times the size of any lion she had seen in any book and came and sat in the circle, staring at her curiously.

The Great Wombat was as big as an African hippopotamus.

The Great Kangaroo was twice the height of her father and stood intimidating and muscular.

The Great Thunderbird had brilliant orange plumage and was even taller than the kangaroo sitting on his haunches.

And last slithered in the great Python, as thick as a

tree trunk and infinitely long, forked tongue tasting the air.

They all stood in the semicircle around Vidya, and she felt their gazes on her like a heavy blanket. And now that they stood here, she didn't know quite what to do.

"Only the Fae monarch may call upon the Old Ones, Vidya," came a whisper of a voice coming from the Great Echidna.

Vidya froze in place. That was true, only the King or Queen of the land could call upon the old ones.

"H-how did I get here then?" she asked uncertainly.

"We would also like to know this," boomed the Great Kangaroo in a voice that made Vidya jump a little. "And I would also like to know where you got this petal from."

Vidya swallowed and tried to explain it as best she could. "The Fae kingdom is in danger. The adults have fallen into a magical sleep. And I have just learned that it is because the Flower of Awakening has been taken by the Bunyips and drained of its power. They have wings now and want to wage war on us. They want revenge."

She was met with silence. A wind rustled the feathers of the Great Thunderbird.

The Great Python let out a hiss. "King Fern sought our counsel two hundred years ago," he hissed. "We knew that solution would not last forever."

"Summer may follow spring," boomed the Great Thunderbird. "But winter must follow autumn."

"There is still the matter of the monarch," grumbled the Great Lion.

"Let us fix that immediately," said the Great Platypus lightly.

"We announce," said the Great Echidna. "Thee Vidya as Fae Queen of the Eastern Bushland Realm, until such time as your father returns to assume his throne."

Vidya stood there, stunned. Pancake let out a soft 'wow'.

The Great Thunderbird suddenly turned his head toward the sky and let out an almighty piercing call that made the hairs on Vidya's arms stand up straight. The earth beneath them began to tremble, and in the middle of the semi-circle, the grass began to fall in upon itself, the very earth collapsing to make a small hole. Inside the newly created dip in the earth, something glinted silver.

The Great Kangaroo bounded powerfully up to the hole and bent low, picking up the shiny object. He turned toward Vidya, who gasped when she saw was it was.

A tiara of stunning filigree silver and pink diamonds sparkled in the sunlight. Without a sound, the Great Kangaroo bounded up to Vidya in a single leap and laid the tiara on her head. Up close, he smelled like flowers and sunlight, his russet fur wasn't one colour at all but a mixture of colours. The Great Kangaroo turned and assumed his position in the circle, and Vidya saw her own reflection in Pancake's eyes as he looked up at her.

"Queen of the Fae," he whispered.

Vidya took a shuddering breath as she tried not to think about it. In her eyes, her father was still the King.

She cleared her throat.

"I need to know what to do," she said. "How do I fix the Fae magic?"

"You have one goal here as I see it, Queen Vidya," hissed the Python. "You must re-charge the Flower of Awakening. Give her back the power that has been drained from her."

"You must recreate the conditions that woke it up thousands of years ago, when she brought the Fae to life," said the Great Wombat.

"How do I do that? What woke it up the first time? When it woke up the Fae?"

"None are living now who were there to see it," whispered the Great Echidna.

"There is one." They all turned toward the Great Lion. "The King of Trees. The Wollemi Pine King. He was there. He will know."

11

PLANS

The Fae King and Queen are the Keeper of Keepers. For a task so grand as this, they are given two gifts. The first is that they are given the obedience of all the plants on the earth. And second, is the creation of a plant of their own choosing.

—The Book of the Fae, Queen Mab the First, 3333 B.C.

W hen Vidya woke up, she knew that she was no longer in the Old Country. That feeling of majesty in the air, the sweet, heavy smell of something grand and important was not there anymore.

Pancake grunted beside her. She lifted herself out of the base of the large tree she had been snuggled up in and stretched out her arms, looking around. Something heavy shifted on her head, and she lifted her hand up to touch it. She felt the hard edges of the tiara against her fingers, and the memory of what had happened flooded in her mind. She would have to marvel at it later because she had to get them home to safety first.

"Where are we?" Pancake said in a hushed voice.

Vidya was asking herself the same question. She peered through the trees. The air was bright and light here, nothing like deep in the dark parts of the Fae forest.

She turned around and studied the tree they had been sleeping under. It was a Eucalyptus tree she knew very well.

"Oh, this is the portal tree to the Blue Mountains, Pancake!" she said with a broad smile. "I am so happy we're here, I honestly thought we'd be deep in the Forbidden Zone where Jimmy threw us."

"So lucky!" cried Pancake happily before Vidya shushed him with a finger.

"We still have to be careful, Pancake, there is a still a Bunyip army roaming about here, remember?"

"Bunyips with wings," said Pancake darkly.

Vidya sighed. How could she have forgotten? She really hoped Lobey got away from the one that followed her up into the trees. The Bunyips were fast learners. How long before they got good enough to fly over the bottomless sky? Vidya swallowed the hard lump in her throat. She was thirsty and hungry and incredibly tired. But at least they didn't have to walk too far.

Pancake climbed back onto her shoulder, and they

trudged slowly through the long grass around the portal tree, listening for any signs of Bunyips.

But this time, they reached the edge of the forest without any incidents. The sun was high in the sky, and Vidya squinted across the gap to the palace, trying to see if there were any signs of anything bad happening. She saw two bright specs roving about the front gardens.

"Let's go home, Pancake," smiled Vidya, and she fluttered her tired wings and, feeling the cool wind on her face, zoomed straight over the Bottomless Sky toward the palace.

She heard the shout before she saw where it came from.

Two Fae kids armed with bows and quivers of arrows slung over their shoulders were waving at her from the end of the path. One of them lifted what looked like a horn to his lips and blew into it with two blasts, one short and one long. *Honk Hooooonk.*

As Vidya touched down, her magenta wings drooped and felt numb. Her legs felt like weak twigs, ready to snap at any moment. She urged them to walk forward. The two Fae kids gaped at her as she passed, but she didn't have the energy to say anything to them.

"Oh my god, Vidya!" Vidya heard Lobey's voice and lifted her tired eyes up toward the palace. Lobey was running toward her, electric blue hair streaming in a mess behind her. There were tears streaming down her face and dark circles under her eyes. Luna and Willow emerged from the palace doors behind her and pelted down the path. Lobey flew into Vidya, wrapping her arms so tightly around her that the tired girl squealed.

"Too tight, too tight!" squeaked Pancake.

Lobey laughed and let them go, wiping tears from her eyes. "Oh, Mother Earth, I thought you were gone for sure." And then her eyes went up to Vidya's head where the silver tiara sat, and her mouth fell open. She pointed a finger at it, eyes wide. "That! That!"

"They made me Queen," explained Vidya tiredly. "I don't deserve it, but they said because my father is asleep, I have to—" Vidya only shrugged to finish her sentence. "I just really need some rest, guys, I've been through the roughest time."

They parted in silence to let her through.

"Tell us everything!" said Lobey, her face contorted with concern—a new expression for her. "What happened in there? I've set a guard—"

"That's good, Lobey, that's great," said Vidya tiredly. Sleep was the only thing on her mind right now.

Bleary-eyed, she trundled through the palace and flew up the stairs straight into her bedroom.

Lily and Daisy were in there, gasping when they saw her, but she didn't have the energy to acknowledge them, all she could do when she reached her bed was flop right down on it, face first.

She was asleep before she hit the mattress.

The group of Fae kids gathered in the room's doorway behind her. Luna and Toad pushed past Lotus and Willow and walked up to Vidya, pulling off her shoes. Lobey helped them tug off her jacket and pulled the covers up and around her, making sure Pancake was settled safely next to her. They stood over her, staring at the sparkling tiara slumped against her pink curls that they all knew had clearly come from another world entirely.

"I don't want to touch it," whispered Luna to her sisters.

Lobey reached a hand out but pulled it back quickly with a shudder.

It was Toad who gently took the tiara off Vidya's head with both hands and laid to rest on her side table. They stared at it for a moment before Willow cleared his throat, and they all woke up out of their daydream and filed out of the room, closing the door quietly behind them.

"What do you think happened to her," asked Lotus, his yellow wings gave a twitch of unease. "She wasn't hurt, was she?"

"No," Lobey shook her head. "But whatever it was, she's lucky to be alive."

In her dream, Vidya found herself in a room made of shadows.

Vidya, she heard a familiar wispy voice. The same voice she had heard when she picked up the golden petal under the sea.

"Hello?" she whispered into the dark.

Then a small section of the shadows parted, and a tiny speck of yellow light appeared. Vidya recognised it immediately. She willed herself closer to it. She needed to get closer.

Gradually, the light grew larger, and from the glow, the form of a gigantic flower emerged. The Flower of Awakening was huge. At least five times the size of any flower Vidya had ever seen. If Vidya had opened her arms on either side of herself, the flower would have been just slightly larger still. Many golden yellow petals unfurled from the centre in layers, creating a beautiful, flowing effect. Golden and silvery veins lined each petal, giving off their own light. But this time, Vidya noticed the light looked duller, softer, sleepier. As if the flower was exhausted. And when the flower spoke to her in her mind, she spoke with a softer voice, as if she was too afraid to speak… or too weak.

"Vidya you... found me," she whispered.

Vidya swore her heart grew in her chest. She wanted nothing more than to help the flower, ease its pain, give it what it needed. Vidya felt the backs of her eyes burn, and she felt like she wanted to cry.

"I'm here," she spoke hurriedly. She felt like time was running out. How long would the vision last for? "I'm trying to help you… to get your energy back somehow. The Old Ones said we have to make it like it was when you first woke us up. Tell me how to do it. Please!" she begged.

"My memory is failing. I cannot remember. There was fire.... but much more, I cannot... I am weak, too weak."

"It's okay, I'll try to find out. The Wollemi Pine, King of the Trees, might be able to help. They said he was there."

"Was he? He was... I cannot... remember..."

Vidya gulped, her heart racing in her chest. This was not looking good.

"The Bunyips... took too much from me. I fear if you do not hurry, it will be the end of me."

"And then what happens?" whispered Vidya.

"And that will be the end of the Fae."

And then everything faded into shadow again, and Vidya slept and slept and slept.

* * *

When Vidya woke up, she yawned loudly and stretched out her aching muscles. Looking out the window, the sun was still high in the sky. Lobey dozed in the window bed, an open book lying on her chest.

"How long did I sleep for?" Vidya asked herself.

Lobey awoke with a startled snort. She breathed deeply and looked out the window, scratching her cheek. "You're finally up! You arrived yesterday."

"That's a long time," frowned Vidya, looking over to see Pancake wide awake, reclining on the pillow next to her, a bowl of blueberries balanced on his round belly.

"Then again, you did almost die," said Lobey darkly.

"You were thrilled to see me," said Vidya with a smile, rolling off the bed stiffly.

"Of course I was," said Lobey, swinging her legs down from the bed and crossing her arms. "I *left you* and fled, saving myself. What type of Fae does that make me?"

Vidya smiled sadly at Lobey. "A smart one."

Lobey scratched the back of her head and sighed. "I thought you were gone, Vidya."

"I thought you'd be happy being *Queen*," teased Vidya.

Lobey threw her hands up in the air and scoffed. "I show you one ounce of niceness, and off you go with it."

Vidya laughed. "Call a meeting," she said. "I'm going to take a bath, then we all need to talk."

"Pancake wouldn't tell us anything," complained Lobey. "No matter how much I poked him."

Vidya smiled at her best friend. "We've been through a lot together, him and I, of course, his loyalty is only to me."

"Alright, well hurry up then."

A squeaky clean Vidya and Pancake met the group: the triplets, Daisy, Lotus, Willow, and Lily, in the palace library. She was immediately swamped with cries of "Vidya!" and "Pancake!" and many pairs of arms were thrown vigorously around her. Her face smooshed in a yellow wing that could only be Lily's, she laughed.

"Let her go," called Lobey, "She's just come back from the dead you know."

They all hastily released her and took back their seats, Daisy pushing a bowl of broccoli stew into her hands. Vidya put it down hastily and picked up a lumpy looking purple muffin instead. But Luna lingered by her side. "Where is your tiara?" she said softly.

Vidya had left it in its place on her side table.

"Well, I can't be wearing that around all the time, can I? It's not practical."

Luna giggled and went to sit back down.

"Spill the beans," said Lobey, "You've kept us waiting long enough."

Vidya nodded and recounted the story from when Lobey had flown away and Jimmy had taken Pancake and Vidya and pelted deep into the forest, eventually flinging them away and how they found themselves in the Old Country. She revealed what they had told her. Pancake filled in with sound effects, like hissing when the great Python hissed or miming how the great Kangaroo placed the crown on Vidya's head.

"So we have to go back into the Fae forest!" groaned Willow.

Lotus whooped with joy, shaking his fist in the air. "Let's do it!" he cried.

"Yes," said Vidya. "Unfortunately, the King of Trees is deep in the forest, and he is the only one who knows how to fix the Flower of Awakening."

"And we need to do all this before the Bunyips figure out how to fly over the gap to the palace," said Lobey. "The one that came after me tumbled right back into the trees. He almost got me, but not quite."

"There are maps in here," said Lotus. "Master Sunny showed us at the start of the year."

"Well, we mustn't be up to that in our class," said Lobey irritably, walking over to the Book Tree.

They all watched as Lobey stomped up to the little Bonsai on his table of cards.

"Book Tree, I need a good map of the Fae forest. Where the Wollemi King lives."

The Bonsai shook his leaves vigorously, then went still.

Lobey turned to gape at them. "Is he saying *no* to me?" she asked, affronted.

"Book Tree, we are in mortal danger! Tell me where the maps to the Wollemi Pine are!"

The Book Tree shook his leaves angrily again.

"He won't give them to us," said Lotus. "Kids aren't allowed to go into the forest, remember?"

"Why didn't you tell me before?" grumbled Lobey, stomping back to her seat.

Lotus shrugged and smirked. "I just wanted to see you try."

"Very funny."

"But Vidya is Queen now," came Luna's soft voice. "And the Queen's word is law."

Silence seeped into the room like heavy smoke, and it weighed on Vidya's shoulders. But she took a deep breath and remembered the great Kangaroo putting the tiara on her head. She strode over to the Book Tree.

"Book Tree, I have a quest that needs to get me to the King of Trees. The Wollemi Pine. Give me a map to him, please."

The Book Tree bent a little as if bowing and plucked out a single card from his box. Vidya held it up triumphantly, and Lotus whooped with joy, running up to her and plucking the card out of her hand and sprinting into the stacks where the maps were kept.

"Got it!" he said, running back and waving a large square of green leaf paper in the air. He spread it out on the table in the middle, and they all craned their heads to look at it.

"So where does the King of all Trees live?" asked Toad.

"There," pointed Willow with his sharp eyes.

"Oh no," said Lobey darkly.

THE KING OF TREES

Of all the sacred trees in the Fae forest, the Wollemi Pine reigns as King. He was there at the turn of the world, watching us as we emerged from the earth. Watching as beings came and left the earth. The quiet observer, the quiet knower of things. If there is one who has seen, it is He.

—The Book of the Fae, Queen Mab the First, 3333 B.C.

The King of Trees, the Wollemi Pine, had put himself in the most protected of locations. Right in the middle of a Cassowary commune. Cassowaries were usually solitary birds, but they had made an exception in the case of the King of Trees. Known as the most dangerous birds alive, they were ferocious and protective, capable of reaching fast speeds and causing real damage in a fight.

Whoever had drawn the map had written, "DO

NOT CROSS" in capital letters and red ink. The cassowaries were clearly bad news. It was too bad they'd have to go there and find that out for themselves.

"Oh, for Earth's sake!" exclaimed Willow, throwing his hands up in the air. "It just had to be in the middle of the most dangerous thing in the world, didn't it?"

"Well, it looks like the cassowaries have been serving the Wollemi King for millions of years," said Lobey, running a finger across the page of a thick black book she had found. "The birds are living dinosaurs, they were around before most of the creatures of the Forbidden Zone."

"Great. Just great," grumbled Willow.

"You'll be fine," stressed Lobey. "Vidya is Fae Queen now, they'll have to listen to her."

The next morning, they set off across the bottomless sky, back into the forest. This time, Vidya, Lotus, and Lily also had bows and arrows, just like Willow, and Lotus had given Pancake a sharp rock to keep 'just in case'. The Bunyips were too strong and clever to risk anymore incidents. If they were to be attacked again, they would get away, even if it meant shooting the things. They branched-hopped with Willow in the lead, as his eyes were the sharpest, and Lotus at the back, as he would be best in a fight if anyone came at them from behind.

They followed the map deep into the forest, and the four children watched their surroundings as it gradually changed. Within the hour, they came to the boundary. Thousands of years ago, an old Fae Queen had, with the permission of each tree, carved out an 'X' in their trunks and painted it red. It was a silent, serious reminder of the danger that awaited them. Willow, having reached the boundary first, paused to stare, his wings standing to attention. Vidya fluttered to join him on his branch.

"This is the furthest any of us have ever been into the forest," he whispered. "Except you, of course."

"Oh, it wasn't that bad," joked Vidya, swatting him on his arm. She couldn't even remember crossing the boundary with Jimmy the other night. He had been going much too fast.

Lily fluttered next to Vidya.

"What's the holdup?" she asked. "Look," she pointed to the forest floor beneath them.

Squinting, Vidya heard Willow take a sharp breath. "Bunyip tracks."

"They're everywhere," admitted Lily. "All over the place."

Ice trickled down Vidya's spine. "How fresh are they?"

Lily's shoulders moved up and down as she took a deep breath. "Recent, within the last hour."

"Let's keep moving then," Vidya replied.

"We're just walking further *in* to danger," Willow muttered under his breath. He made to move onto the next tree, but Vidya placed a hand on his chest.

"Willow," she hissed. "I had a dream about the Flower of Awakening the other night."

He met her eyes with startled ones. "And do you know what she told me?"

"What?" he whispered.

"If we don't restore her magic, the Fae are dead. Forever," she poked him in the chest. "Stop complaining, and let's do what we need to do, okay?"

She watched Willow as his navy wings drooped with guilt. He swallowed. "I know Vidya, I'm sorry. I want to help as much as anyone else."

"I know, Will," she said kindly. "Let's just keep moving, hey?"

He nodded and took off for the next tree, waving the others to follow. They branch-hopped through the forest for the next hour without anything serious happening, but Vidya could not shake a creepy feeling itching at her, like insects crawling in her belly, that danger was all around them.

The trees grew closer and closer together, which meant that the canopy overhead let in less and less light. Eventually, the trees clustered so close to one another that the branches and leaves overlapped above them, closing the canopy completely. The kids had to squint through the darkness, and it gave the air a sort of heavy, sinister feeling. Nothing moved in the forest around them, no birds flit through the trees, and no small animals pushed through the leaf litter in the moist earth below. The kids found it hard to breathe the heavy moist air that had the mild smell of rotting fruit.

They stopped almost a dozen times to check the map. They were all nervous, jumping at random sounds, like when the wind rustled a branch or made a whistling noise between the trees. And they found it difficult to keep track of the landmarks they were supposed to be following. They turned left at the banana shaped tree but realised too late that they had missed the patch of monstrous pumpkins, mistaking them for large rocks. They had to double back to stay on the right track, but this type of thing went on and on for hours. Her father's words rang clear in her ears the entire time. *'Always be alert in the Fae forest, Vidya, there's no telling what could happen.'*

They had been travelling along in silence for a few minutes when Willow raised his hand up in the air so abruptly, he almost fell off the branch he was on. His arms wheeled frantically through the air before he steadied himself.

Vidya froze, one hand on the trunk of her own tree, when she saw them. Two enormous shapes shifted on the ground below. Bunyips. The four children froze on their branches, wondering what to do. Had they walked into a trap? But the Bunyips showed no sign of noticing them. Just as Vidya was turning to signal to Lotus to move away from there, they heard two gravelly voices like rocks grating together, having a conversation.

"Do you smell that?" said one.

Snuffling sounds came from one of the Bunyips below.

"Nah, smell nothing," the other replied.

Vidya noticed they spoke slowly, speaking the words as if they were new and unusual to their mouths.

She imagined that talking through a mouthful of very large teeth would be difficult.

"It smells like Fae," grumbled the first. "Sweet and sticky and yummy smelling."

"Nar, all I smell is you," replied the other.

"When do you think we'll make a move?"

"What are you talking about?"

"When did the King say we're launching our attack? I can fly really well now, I think."

"I don't know."

"You never listen! I think it was supposed to be in three nights' time. When the moon is sleeping in the sky."

"When is the moon sleeping in the sky?"

"When it's a new moon, you dolt. That means there's no moon in the sky. Geez, the Flower of Awakening skipped you a little bit, hey."

"Leave me alone," complained the other. "I'm hungry."

"No problems there. In three nights, you'll get to eat all the Fae you can fit into your huge tummy."

They began laughing, an awful, grating, throaty noise that made the kids listening above, cringe. Vidya cast a look behind her to where Lily was frozen on her branch, her eyes huge. Lotus was next to her, his bow knocked with an arrow ready to shoot. Vidya waved her arms at him frantically. *No!* She mouthed at him. *No!* She finally caught his eye without falling out of the tree herself, and he guiltily lowered his bow, but didn't return the arrow. He shrugged and mouthed *just in case*. Vidya rolled her eyes and shook her head. The

Bunyips were now loping off in the opposite direction to the way the Fae were travelling. With a sigh of relief, Willow led them out of danger to the next tree and away from the huge black monsters.

They continued along, passing many unusual sights. There was a creek full of glowing rocks, trees that grew upside down and on top of each other, and weirder still, at one stage, they saw rocks that were fighting each other, hurling themselves at one another aggressively, until one of them burst into a shower of crumbs. They stopped to watch this last event for a few minutes before shaking their heads at one another, checking the map, and moving on, realising they were quite close to the home of the Wollemi King. Willow reminded them they should be more wary if there were ferocious cassowaries lurking nearby.

The dense trees did not let them see too far ahead, so it was a rather big shock when they saw bright light streaming through the trees in the distance. When they reached the beams of light, they found the forest encircled by an enormous clearing with bright green short grass that spread out for acres.

Crouched behind a few bushes bordering the clearing, the Fae children and Pancake gasped.

In the centre of the clearing, on a small hill in front of them, stood the largest tree Vidya had ever seen. Whatever she had pictured a million-year-old tree to look like, it was not this. Its trunk plunged into the blue sky, so tall that she was sure it was at least three times as tall as any tree she'd seen before. There were many branches extending from the central trunk, but each branch did not split into more branches. He reminded Vidya of a fern, with many long, slender, green leaves extending from each branch. He looked lush and healthy, and regal, just as a King should, Vidya decided.

But between them and the King of Trees sat an impressive group of ten to twenty large cassowaries, lounging like giant grey rocks on the grass. They were emu shaped birds, good sized, long, feathered bodies, brilliant blue necks, with a small head crowned with their famous bony crest. Long legs ended in huge, powerful feet that were known to be able to kill a grown man with a single kick.

"These are northern cassowaries," whispered Lotus, peering at them. "And female. They're bigger than the males. Look at that one," he said, pointing at the largest. "That lady must be two meters tall, even taller than your father, Vidya."

Vidya cleared her throat. "Well, we'd better go and have a chat with them."

"What do you mean *have a chat?*" Willow hissed, affronted. But there was no point, Vidya had already stood up and was now striding toward the group of cassowaries. The other kids hastily followed her, exclaiming at her boldness. Pancake grumbled in her pocket but did not comment, clutching tightly onto the fabric.

The cassowaries did not seem surprised to see them. They lounged in their spots as Vidya approached, watching her every move with beady black eyes. The largest of them stood and casually strolled over the grass to meet her at the edge of the group.

"Hello," said Vidya a little breathlessly. Now that she was here, she didn't quite know what to say. "I… er… seek an audience with the King of Trees."

"The Wollemi Pine King!" corrected the cassowary, in a surprisingly deep voice, looking down her beak at her. "The Greatest and Oldest! King of all that grows under the sun!"

"Well, yes," said Vidya awkwardly, feeling the others gather behind her. "He has information that I desperately need."

"So!" the cassowary said loudly. "I am Akurra, leader of the cassowaries who guard the Wollemi Pine King. Glory be upon him. *I* will decide whether or not you get to see him!"

"But he's just there," Lotus pointed to the enormous tree towering above them all just ten meters away.

Akurra ignored him. "So, what do you have?" she asked. "What have you brought us?"

Vidya paused in confusion. "Er… nothing?"

"Then!" Akurra announced. "You are not permitted entry," she fluffed her feathers arrogantly. "Leave, or suffer the consequences. My girls are quite hungry and like the taste of Fae children."

Lotus gaped at her.

"You are speaking to the Queen of the Eastern Bushland Fae!" he said. "And the Queen's word is law!"

"That may be," droned Akurra, unimpressed. "However, you are no longer in what you call *the Safe Zone*.

Here, the King of Trees is ruler. You are not permitted entry until you bring us what we desire."

"And what would that be?"

"The most valuable thing you have."

The kids all exchanged incredulous looks.

"Seriously?" scoffed Willow. "What a thing to ask!"

"What about him?" Akurra lowered her neck to peer at Vidya's tummy. She realised Akurra meant Pancake.

"He's not for sale!" Vidya retorted, covering Pancake defensively with her hand.

"Well, off you go then," said Akurra, jerking her head for them to leave. "And don't return until you have something nice to give me."

The kids had no choice but to turn around and continue back the way they had come. They flopped down on the grass, groaning about their sore legs and wings. Akurra had gone back to sit in the sun with the rest of the group and didn't seem to mind the Fae kids sitting at the edge of the clearing.

"What a rude bird," remarked Lily, pulling her backpack into her lap.

Lotus and Willow pulled out a couple of muffins Daisy and Luna had given them and wolfed them down hungrily.

Vidya was rummaging through her bag for some food for herself when she saw it. The crystal vial of silvery liquid. She remembered who had given it to her.

The most valuable thing you own…

Vidya jumped up and ran back over to the group of Cassowaries, waving the vial in the air.

Akurra stood back up and lumbered over, her eyes narrowed.

"What is that?" she snapped.

"The most valuable thing anyone will ever give you, Akurra," said Vidya, confidently, showing her the vial. "Unicorn Tears. From the only living unicorn. Princess Sonakshi of the Blue Mountains and Macuata," said Vidya. "Take a drop and you'll have the power of a unicorn for a day."

Akurra's eyes grew so big Vidya thought they would pop out. She smirked triumphantly. As valuable as the tears were, being a friend to a unicorn meant Vidya could just get more later if she needed. But to anyone else, these tears were priceless.

"That is something," breathed Akurra. She waved another cassowary over with her wing, and the other bird hurried over, reached down and gently took the vial from her hand with her beak. "Back in my day, many a unicorn walked the land, we'll be glad to accept this gift."

Vidya nodded.

"Well then," said Akurra, regarding Vidya with a new respect. "Come on. The King will be eager to see you."

Vidya turned and waved for the others who were staring at her, gaping. There would be time to explain later.

They followed Akurra over the grass up to the base of the enormous tree.

"Your Majesty," bowed Akurra.

Vidya stared up into the branches and gave a slight

bow of her head too, urging her pounding heart to slow down. Her mother had always taught her that when speaking to a tree, the most polite thing to do was to keep your eye steady at the topmost part of the trunk you could see below the first branches. Pancake climbed out of Vidya's pocket and clambered up onto her shoulder, craning his neck to look at the oldest tree any one of them had ever seen.

And then a voice spoke, and none of the children had ever heard a voice so deep and regal as that of the King of Trees.

"Who are you?" They felt the voice rumble in the ground under their feet, and it rose up their legs to vibrate in their chests. But although the voice was heavy with age and wisdom, Vidya felt it was rather soft with kindness too.

Vidya shuddered. "I… I am the Fae queen of the Eastern Bushland, your majesty."

His great leaves rustled, although there was no wind.

"I was there the day your kind were woken from the earth," he rumbled gently. "Tell me what it means to be Fae, my Queen, and I will give you the knowledge you desire."

Vidya frowned and chewed her lip. An image of her Nani came into her mind's eye. How she fearlessly cared for the Devil's Fingers when no one else could. She thought of the Flower of Awakening and how the Fae magic looked after the plants.

"The Fae are the guardians of the plants," said Vidya

confidently. "We care for the plants when no one else will."

The Wollemi Pine King remained still and unmoving. Vidya's stomach did a little flip. Had she said the wrong thing?

But his voice rumbled through the ground again. "What is your name, Queen of the Fae?"

"Um… Vidya."

"Ah! Queen Vidya. Tell me, do you know what your name means?"

Vidya was slightly taken aback, but her mother had, of course, told her what her name meant many times. It had been chosen by her Nani, from her home country, India. "In Hindi, Vidya means knowledge."

"Not just any knowledge," rumbled the King. "Knowledge of the highest kind, the truest kind. If this knowledge wore a dress, it would be pure white. Queen Vidya, look inside yourself *and tell me what it means to be Fae.*"

"To be Fae…" started Vidya. Her mind raced. She knew she was missing something, but what was it?

But it was Willow who finished her sentence. "It means to see all living things as yourself. To be Fae means to see all plants and animals and beings as one."

"Ahhh," breathed the King of Trees. "The Fae, are nothing if not loyal to one another. How I have missed the Fae in my little corner of the world. I accept this answer from the boy with hair like twilight."

Vidya could not help but turn to Willow and smile, he grinned in return.

"What is it you seek?" he rumbled kindly. "Although I believe I think I may know."

Vidya cleared her throat. "You were there that day the Flower of Awakening woke up the Fae?"

"I was."

"The Flower of Awakening is drained of her power. I need to know how she woke up last time. What made her awaken the Fae, and how do we restore her power once again?"

The gigantic tree rustled his leaves in memory.

"The Wollemi were there when the Flower of Awakening sung her song for the first time. Except we did not call her that—I knew her by another name at that time. When she awoke, we spoke back to her and told her of the kingdom above the sea. If she is to be restored, she must feel my presence and remember. I will give you a spell thus: Take my wood and give it to your finest Bowyer. They must make a bow and an arrow. With this bow and a single arrow, you must deliver the spark."

"What do you mean by spark?"

He quivered, "The thing that the plant Kingdom despises the most. Fire."

"Fire?"

"Earth fire. That day, it flew across the sky."

"What type of earth fire flies across the sky?" asked Vidya, looking behind her.

"A comet," said Willow breathlessly, "It had to be. It was a comet that awoke the Flower of Awakening."

"This is all you will require," rumbled the Wollemi Pine.

The King of Trees shook himself, and three long lengths of wood tumbled down to the ground. Willow hurriedly scooped them up, holding them against his body reverently.

"Thank you, your Majesty," bowed Vidya.

"You are most welcome, my Queen," he replied, rustling his branches. "Please do visit with me again, with your little quokka."

As they walked back toward her, Akurra watched them with curious eyes.

"We do not often see your kind here," she drawled, looking at them all one by one.

"No, this is a sort of emergency," Vidya replied.

"Of what kind?"

"Of the war kind. An army of Bunyips is out to kill us."

Akurra jerked a little in surprise. "Interesting," she remarked. "How things can change so quickly."

"Yes, well, thanks for your help," Vidya replied, turning away. "We'll be getting on our way now."

"A word of advice, Fae Queen," Akurra said, making Vidya stop in her tracks. "When at war with an unusual enemy, one must think unusually."

Vidya turned and gave Akurra a curt nod before following the others out of the clearing.

1 3
YARA-MA-YHA-WHO

Foolish is he who walks into a dragon's den. Foolish is he who walks into the Fae forest. For with either, none survive without the scars to tell the tale.

—The Book of the Fae, Queen Mab the First, 3333 B.C.

The team branch-hopped out of the Wollemi King's territory and back into the darkness of the forest. After the clean open air the and the cassowaries lived in, it was such a shame they would have to retreat back into the uncomfortable, humid darkness again.

Consulting their map, they decided to head back to the palace where it would be safe to talk about their next move. Willow agreed to make the bow and prepare the arrow out of the wood the King had given them. He was the finest whittler of them all, having the sharp eyes for such work. Lily offered to prepare the string for the bow from her guardian plant, the Black-wood tree, which was well suited for bowstrings.

There was still the matter of the 'earth fire', the 'spark' that the Tree King had spoken of. The bow was meant to deliver that light to the Flower of Awakening to re-charge her power. At the dawn of time, it had been a comet, a ball of earth and fire flying through the sky that had done it. But how were they supposed to get a comet this time?

"Did anyone see that?" Willow whispered suddenly.

Vidya joined Willow on his branch and squinted into the darkness. "No, what was it?"

"You know my vision is good, Vidya, don't you?" he whispered uncertainly.

"Yes, the best."

Willow rubbed his eyes and frowned. Shaking his head. "I honestly thought I saw a… koala riding a toad like a horse. He had a saddle and everything."

Vidya covered her mouth to stifle a laugh. "E-excuse me?" she stuttered. Pancake let out a little giggle from his place peeking out of her pocket.

Willow smiled, embarrassed, and shook his head. "Honestly… I really think I did. But they disappeared into the darkness quickly." He pointed at a spot just ahead.

Vidya squinted into the distance, then cast a glance backward at Lotus and Lily waiting behind them.

Willow cast a glance backward as well. "Don't tell the others."

"I'm just going to pretend you didn't say anything at all," Vidya rubbed her arms, now covered in goosebumps. "Did you see anything?" whispered Vidya at Pancake.

"No koala," Pancake shook his head. "And Toad is back home."

Vidya snorted. "Yes, she is. She'll love this story though."

"Well, whatever it was, I hope it's the friendly sort," muttered Willow.

Vidya pulled at a magenta curl of her own hair. She did *not* need to say that anything in the darkest part of the forest was not going to be the 'friendly sort'.

She prodded Willow to keep going. With another squint into the darkness, he shrugged and fluttered to the next branch.

Suddenly, Lotus let out a choked cry, followed by a *thump* sound. Vidya whirled around to see Lily trying to scramble up the tree she was on, while Lotus was lying on his back on the ground below, a heavy rope around his ankles and four small, red, dwarf sized men surrounding him.

"Yarama!" Lotus cried. "Fly!"

The little red men cackled evilly, ignoring Lotus' attempts to free himself.

Willow let out a cry that was immediately cut short as Vidya watched a thin black rope with a rock tied on the end of it fly toward him, wrapping itself around his ankles. It was yanked so hard that he was hurled toward the ground. Vidya immediately leapt into the air, trying to get higher up into the trees. But she didn't get far before she felt a rope snake around her ankles and tighten painfully.

"No!" she gasped, flapping her wings hard, trying to get away by the sheer force of her upward lift. The tug on her ankles was not as strong as her wings pulling her upward. If she could just try harder… suddenly, the force on her ankles increased, and she heard the Yarama chanting beneath her.

"Heave! Heave! Heave!"

When she looked down, no less than four Yarama were pulling on the rope leading to her ankles. And with each heave, she was pulled through the air, down, down, down. Next to her, Lily was being pulled in the same way. Vidya thought quickly, and without warning him, grabbed Pancake from her pocket and threw him up toward the trees. "Run, Pancake!" she called, hoping she had aimed well.

By the time she felt small hands reaching for her feet, her wings were aching and sore. They drooped, and she was thrown onto solid ground.

She lifted her head. Willow, Lily, and Lotus lay on their backs, protesting loudly next to her, Pancake was nowhere to be seen. Vidya's heart leapt. He must've gotten away! What great luck. Perhaps he could… *what*? Vidya thought. Go back to the palace and get help? They were too deep in the forest for that. Vidya gazed into the trees above her for any signs of Pancake's furry round form but was quickly distracted by the Yarama standing over her, jeering.

"Looky here," jeered one. "We gots Fae childreys!"

Vidya had never seen a Yara-ma-yha-who up close, except in the chalkboard sketches Master Sunny had drawn for them. And she had to admit though, the real-life things were a lot worse to look at it.

They were the size of small children, shorter than Vidya by a full head. Their skin was a rusty red colour, with bald heads, long skinny arms and legs, and true to Master Sunny's word, on the palm of each hand were tiny, shiny suckers, like the ones an octopus has, only dirty looking. They all wore the same dirty little shorts and smelled like Mahiya's diaper, but much, much worse. Vidya couldn't tell which ones were boys and which ones were girls. They all looked exactly the same.

"Let us go!" demanded Lotus angrily, struggling against the five Yarama that were binding him with black ropes.

"Oooh, the Fae childreys are angry," taunted one Yarama, pulling a rope taut. "Nope, no letting go. We're off to our chief! He will be so happy."

They repeated the action with Willow, Lily, and Vidya, who fought and flailed as much as they could, but the little men were far stronger and meaner than they looked. The Yarama hauled them to their feet and pulled them along with the ropes, like puppies on a lead. There were ten Yarama in total, and Vidya had no idea how they were going to get out of this.

They were led through the darkness into another part of the forest where a system of caves was spread out. Yarama were scattered everywhere, and when they saw the Fae children, they jumped up and down, cheered, and waved short spears in the air. They were brought into a dark cave lit with tiny burning flowers in holders along the wall. Toward the back, a slightly larger Yarama sat in a chair made out of dried mud, and it was to him the prisoners were brought. Up close, Vidya could see that he wore a little woven hat with a black feather sticking out of it. Vidya guessed this was the chief of the tribe. Behind her, Vidya heard the whole tribe of Yarama filter in. They chattered excitedly. The Chief stood up.

"Who do we have here?" he sneered, beady eyes greedily taking them in.

"You are speaking to the Fae Queen!" yelled Lotus from next to her. "The Queen's word is law!"

"We call the Bunyip King our leader now, Fae child," sneered a nasty-looking Yarama gripping Lotus' arm.

"He has promised to save us from the Leaf Master!" squeaked one.

"That's right," said the Chief defiantly. "From here to the fire flowers of the western marshes, The Leaf Master rules us all. The Bunyip King has promised to give us back our land!"

Next to her, Vidya heard Willow gasp, and she hoped he was okay.

"Can you do that, Fae Queen?" jeered one. "Can *you* take down the biggest nastiest spirit in the deep dark woods?"

"Yeah! Show us what you can do Fae Queen!"

"Show us your magic!"

"Yeah, show us your powers!"

There was a chorus of cackling laughter and pointing figures.

Sweat trickled down Vidya's spine. "I… I…"

Vidya knew she was nothing like her father or mother. She had no guardian plant to speak of and had no powers. Where her father, the real King might have been able to stand up to these monsters, she was in no position to do so.

"Thought so!" shouted one.

"Take their noses!" cried the Chief, punching his fist in the air.

A Yarama advanced toward Vidya, while three others walked toward Lotus, Lily, and Willow, the suckers on their hands pointed right at their faces.

"Noooooo!" she heard Willow cry from next to Lotus.

"Stooop!" Lily cried.

"Wait!" she cried, trying to turn her head away from the Yarama who was now standing in front of her, his brown eyes shining with glee. "No!" But the Yarama pressed his suckers on either side of her nose, and she screwed her eyes shut. Her nose went numb, and Vidya heard a loud *squelch* as her nose was separated from her face. Suddenly, the middle of her face felt very cold. She opened her eyes to find the Yarama gleefully waving her little brown round nose in the air. Vidya now had to breath through her mouth.

"The Queen's nose!" he cried, holding it up so they could all see.

The little red men cheered, clapping their hands above their heads and jumping up and down.

Lily gave a nasally squeal behind her as, with three more squelching sounds, her friends' noses were also taken.

"Give it back!" Lotus shouted. Vidya was turned around by the Yarama holding her and positioned so that she and her friends were in a wide semicircle, with the tribe of Yarama in front of them. Lotus, Lily, and Willow's noses were all absent, replaced by smooth brown skin in the middle of their faces. Vidya couldn't help herself. It started as a giggle, quickly becoming a full belly laugh as Willow's mouth fell open in shock.

"I'm… so… sorry," she laughed, "but… you… all… look ridiculous!"

Lotus clearly couldn't help himself either, because he let out a small nasally chuckle. Vidya looked at the Yarama who were staring at her.

"I'm sorry," she sneered at them. "Is that honestly the best you can do? Steal people's noses?"

The ridiculousness of the situation just made her laugh harder, and the Yarama holding her arms fought to hold her still as she bent over laughing.

"We have an entire Kingdom to save and here you are stealing… our noses!"

The whole thing was stupid, to be sure. But that might have been the worst thing she could say, because the chief Yarama seemed to take that as a challenge.

"Take them to dungeons!" he bellowed angrily. The whole tribe cheered as they were led away by their ropes to the back, outside the cave, toward the gaping hole in the middle of the ground. The four Fae kids quickly learned that they had to breathe through their mouths now that their noses were gone, and it was rather annoying thing to have to do.

They were led down slippery dirt steps into the dark. The Yarama at the front held up a small lantern with a small glowing plant inside of it. It gave off an orangey glow that made the tiny cavern dungeon look even smaller. The Yarama threw them against the dirt walls and tied their ropes around heavy tree roots that protruded through the wall.

"You can't do this!" cried Lotus.

"Yeah, especially with that koala riding that toad out there," mumbled Willow.

That single sentence made all five Yarama in the cave freeze on the spot.

"What did you say?" asked a Yarama in a quiet voice, totally absent of any sneer.

Willow looked up in surprise to find five Yarama staring at him, poised in various states of action.

"I... I saw something in the forest?" he said, trying to speak clearly without his nose.

"What did you see?" asked the same Yarama, stepping closer to him now.

"I... I... saw... a... koala... on a toad," stammered Willow, looking to Vidya for support.

"Alert the chief!" cried the Yarama. "Alert the chief, the Leaf Master is here!"

The Yarama scrambled as fast as they could out of the cave.

The three Fae kids exchanged fearful expressions.

"What could be so scary that even the Yarama are afraid of it?" asked Willow, blowing a raspberry.

"Have you heard of the Leaf Master?" asked Vidya to Lotus.

The older boy shook his blonde head. "Nope, never." He pulled at his ropes, but they held fast.

"I sure hope Pancake is okay," said Vidya. "I hope he's far away from here."

"I don't!" said Willow. "I hope he comes out here and saves us!"

"Willow," groaned Vidya. "But you're right, I hope so too."

"But did you guys see?" Willow said excitedly. "Look at that flower in the lanterns. That Chief Yarama said 'fire flowers of the western marshes!' I saw them on the map!"

"What about them?" asked Vidya glumly, tugging on the black ropes.

"*Fire*," urged Willow. "Fire and earth together! What King Wollemi was talking about!"

Recognition sparked with Vidya. In all the hustle of being captured by the Yarama, she had forgotten why they were even here.

"That's the missing piece of the puzzle!" Vidya exclaimed, clicking her fingers together. "Good one, Willow. That's exactly how we complete the spell."

"Good one, Will," echoed Lily. "But we can't get to the marshes if we're stuck in this place. And it's gone all quiet outside, I wonder what's happening."

They sat in an uneasy silence, mouths open for breathing, for what seemed like forever, listening to the sounds of the Yarama scurrying outside. Very soon, outside, it went quiet. The four prisoners looked at each other fearfully by the orange light of the lantern.

But it wasn't long before a shuffling sound by the entrance made them freeze.

14

FIRE FLOWERS

When met with a dangerous plant, the wisest course of action is to be polite.

—The Book of the Fae, Queen Mab the First, 3333 B.C.

"Is it a ghost?" breathed Lotus.

"Ghosts don't make noises," whispered Willow.

Pancake's brown face appeared around the corner, and the Fae kids groaned with relief.

"Thank the earth, Pancake!" hissed Vidya.

"Why are Yarama so scared?" asked Pancake. "They running back into their cave."

"Oh nothing," said Vidya and Lotus hurriedly.

Pancake cast them a confused look but shook his head.

"Well, lucky Pancake is here," he said pointing to his mouth. "I have very sharp teeth."

It didn't take Pancake long to chomp through the ropes that held them.

"Nice one, Pancake, thank the earth you came back!" said Lily.

"I wasn't gonna leave you here!" he said.

"But come on," said Vidya. "Let's get out of here,"

Vidya grabbed Pancake, shoved him back in her front pocket, and followed Willow, Lotus, and Lily up the dirt stairs into the night air. Not a single Yarama was in sight. The little dirt clearing in front of the cave was empty.

"The air feels weird," said Lotus, rubbing his arms.

A chill had begun to seep into Vidya's chest.

"I have a bad feeling," she said softly.

"Let's get into the cover of the trees," hissed Lily. "The Yarama have gone into hiding, we should too."

They used their wings to flutter themselves quickly across the clearing and into the darkness of the large gnarly trees.

"Up there," they followed Pancake's direction into a large tree with thick brown leaves. All three Fae crouched on a sturdy branch, peering down into the clearing. "This is where I hid while I waited." Pancake said. "Once they put you inside that underground prison, all of a sudden they scrambled out into that big cave."

"That would be Will's doing," whispered Lotus.

"Why?" asked Pancake.

Lotus and Vidya looked at Willow awkwardly.

"I told them I saw something in the forest,"

admitted Willow. "They seemed to think it was this Leaf Master guy."

"Apparently he's being ruling over them," said Vidya. "The Bunyip King promised to get rid of him, so they told us they serve him now."

"Well, I don't know about you guys," hissed Lily, "but I sort of don't feel like hanging around to find out whether he's gonna turn up or not."

"Right," said Lotus. "Which way to the fire marshes?"

"West," Willow pointed to their right. "But wait, what about our noses?"

"Oh right," said Lily, screwing up her face. "But I don't know if it's a good idea to hang—"

The sound of drums reached their ears.

Boom. Boom. Boom.

Their eyes darted around the clearing, looking for the source. Willow silently pointed to a section of the trees on the other side where two small shadows were emerging.

Two large green frogs the size of large dogs hopped out into the clearing. Each held a drum in one front limb, and when they reached the centre of the clearing, they sat there, a wide gap between them, banging on the drums.

Vidya was about to whisper something to the others when a larger shadow hopped into the clearing.

A gigantic, lumpy, brown toad the size of a horse hopped in, a large, round, cloaked figure riding him, gripping reins to control his movements. From within the black cloak was the large furry face of the biggest koala Vidya had ever seen.

Vidya had to cover her mouth to stop herself from gasping. Pancake trembled in her pocket.

The huge toad hopped regally into the centre of the clearing, right between the two smaller frogs. The large, hooded koala figure sat, waiting. Pancake and the four kids held their breaths.

A small movement on the opposite side of the clearing—where the Yarama were hiding in their cave, caught their eye. The Chief Yarama, the black feather on his cap bobbing with each step, ran into the clearing in front of the frogs, something cupped between his hands. He came to a stop a few meters in front of the robed koala and fell onto the ground, lying flat on his tummy. Vidya saw how rapidly the chief was breathing by the rising and fall of his back, and she couldn't but help feel sorry for the creature.

The Koala pulled on the reins, and the gigantic Toad stepped forward over the dirt ground to come to stand over the chief.

"Your tax is due, Yara-ma-yha-who," came a dry, raspy voice.

Vidya's skin crawled.

"I have it! I have it, my Lord!" came the Chief's muffled cry from the dirt. He held out his hands over his head, showing him something.

"I've heard disturbing things, *Chief of the Yarama*," said the voice a little more quickly. "I've heard that you have been speaking to the Bunyip King about me."

"Never, my Lord! Never!" cried the Yarama, his face still pushed into the dirt.

The robed koala titled his head back and laughed, a raspy cackle. Vidya tried to get a good look at his face, but they were too far from their position in the tree.

"Let me tell you one thing, Yarama," sneered the koala. "You will *never be rid of me*."

The Yarama remained silent for only a moment before he spoke into the dirt once more.

"I have four noses for you this month, Leaf Master. *Four!*"

The Leaf Master nodded. "It will do," he said lightly.

The Yarama chief pushed himself off the dirt, moved to stand up, and held out his hands, bowing low.

"Oh no," Pancake whispered from Vidya's pocket as they watched the Leaf Master scoop up their four noses and place them in a pocket of his robe.

"Now," the Leaf Master announced loudly. "I must deal with the four Fae sitting in that tree."

The children did not even discuss it, Lotus was first. He turned, leapt off the tree branch, and hurled himself into the forest, the others frantically following.

They fled into the forest single file, and did not look back. Lotus ran on his fast feet, propelled forward by his yellow wings. Luckily, he had remembered the direction Willow had mentioned just minutes before when he had asked where the western marshes were. The others ran as fast as they could after him until their legs and wings burned. They ran through the darkness, not looking at what they passed, not looking behind them, looking at only what was ahead.

"We should be careful!" panted Willow after about half an hour from second position, his navy wings almost making him disappear in the dark. "We don't know what's—argh!"

Lily, in third position, had just tripped and fallen right into him, causing both of them to fall on top of each other over and over again through the leaves and dirt.

Lotus slowed ahead of them, looking back with a startled frown. Vidya ran forward to help them both up. Willow groaned, rubbing his hip.

"Sorry, Will," grumbled Lily, panting and covered in dirt. "I must've tripped over a root or—"

"No, you fell over me," came a high-pitched squeaky voice from the ground behind them.

Startled, Vidya looked around at their surroundings for the first time. It was incredibly dark, so the four Fae and Pancake squinted around them, trying to see who had spoken and whether they should keep running. But the voice had seemed rather… friendly, if anything. It was a moment before it spoke again.

"Oh, sorry, you can't see me in the dark. I'm over here… no, left… sorry, right… and down!"

They followed his voice, and Vidya, closest to the thing, stepped forward to find a white sturdy mushroom with a tiny mouth and two blinking human eyes staring back at her.

"Oh gosh," she murmured.

"Gosh, yes," it replied shyly. Then looking at Lily, "Sorry about making you fall."

"Sorry, I kicked you, I guess," replied Lily politely.

"Oh, no problem," said the mushroom. "You'll be paying me back anyhow."

Vidya cast a wary glance over her shoulder at the others. She suddenly did not like this mushroom.

"How's that?" she asked carefully.

"When the Bunyip King rules the Eastern Bushland, the Fae will be our servants," said the mushroom smoothly.

They stared at him, and he stared back mildly, an odd smile on his mushroom face. A burning sensation suddenly arose in Vidya's tummy. She stepped up to the mushroom, crouched down, and looked him dead in the eye.

"Yeah? Well, I'm the Fae Queen, little mushroom. And when I win, there will be no Bunyips left. They will forget they even existed."

The mushroom peered back at her in silence for a moment before he spoke.

"Why, then, you are no Fae Queen at all."

Vidya jerked back as if the mushroom had hit her. She blinked, then stood.

"Let's go," she said to the others. "We've already stayed here way to long."

They cast wary eyes about the area but saw no sinister movements in the darkness.

Willow quickly checked the map, and they adjusted their direction and moved on.

. . .

They walked through much of the night, with the adrenaline of the scare of the Leaf Master keeping their tiredness away. Fae wings were not like bird's wings. They were thin and delicate which meant they could not not fly far for long periods of time. So they were left with walking or branch-hopping to get around. They ate left over ripe bananas from Lotus' backpack, and Willow gave them all Bilberries to eat, which supercharged their vision again through the dark forest.

On approach to the marshes, the forest changed. The trees thinned, and the ground became softer. They could see the sky again, and it held the blue-grey light of the coming dawn. Through the big gaps between the trees, the group could see pale wet ground that looked as if it was lit from beneath by a glowing yellow light. The land was dotted with small dark flowers that extended as far as the eye could see.

"Oooh!" whispered Lily. "So pretty."

They came to stand by the last tree, marvelling at the sight of the glowing earth.

"How lucky are we? I wish the others could have seen this," said Lotus. "I've never seen earth glow with light like this."

But Lotus didn't understand half their luck. Because they had no noses, however, what the four Fae kids could not smell was the strong, ever present smell of natural gas. The type that humans use in stoves. The type that explodes when you light it.

"But why are the flowers not lit?" asked Willow, crouching down to look at the closest flower. It sat still and black, snuggled into the wet ground. "These are the same ones the Yarama had in their lanterns."

Lotus walked through the marshes, his boots making a soft squelching sound with each step. The others followed him, curiously looking around at the strange black, leathery flowers.

If they could have smelled the gas in the air, they would've immediately known that what they were doing was a very, very bad idea, and they would've left immediately. As it was, however, the four kids and Pancake, now balanced on Vidya's shoulder wandered further into the golden marshes, entranced by the way their feet made small dents in the glowing earth. Lotus paused in his examinations and crouched, placing his hands into the wet, sandy earth.

"It's warm," he said in surprise, grabbing some of the earth and squelching it in between his hands. He squinted at the ground, peering at it, bent down low. "What is that? Willow, what do your Bilberry eyes see?"

Vidya felt Willow crouch down behind her. Lily had plucked a black flower and was feeling its leaves between her fingers. She raised it to her face to smell it, then realised she didn't have a nose with which to smell and let out a sort of half giggle, half sob.

"It smells weird here," said Pancake watching her, his little black nose twitching in distaste.

"What does it smell like, Pancake?" asked Willow frowning deeply.

"Hmmm," Pancake tapped a finger to his chin. "Not smelled before, but bad."

"Like someone farted bad?" asked Lotus. "Or like something else."

Pancake shook his head. "Not like fart. Just bad."

"Well," said Willow. "Whatever it is beneath the earth, it's shifting, do you see that?"

Vidya squinted at the ground. Beneath the earth, the glow moved unevenly and unpredictably. Vidya was reminded of Mahiya's sparks, the way one of her sparks would move rapidly and make something catch alight. Lily unfurled the map again to study it in the new light. In the distance, the sky began to lighten with the dawn. But then Willow spoke, and it all clicked together.

"This… wet stuff. It's not water," he said with a dark note in his voice.

They all turned to look at him.

He held up the shining liquid he had just rubbed between his fingers. "It's oil."

"Guys…" said Lily quietly, shaking out the map. "There's writing here on the map we didn't see before. Here it says 'natural gases' and the map doesn't call these the western marshes. They're called the 'Western Exploding Marshes'.

"Uh oh!" shouted Vidya. "Run!"

They all turned to run back out the way they came but were immediately stopped.

"Oh, there'll be no running," came a raspy, sinister voice.

15

THE LEAF MASTER

When all seems lost, look up to the sky and look down to the ground and know that while the earth sings her song beneath your feet, you are never alone.

—The Book of the Fae, Queen Mab the First, 3333 B.C.

They had been foolish to think that they had lost the Leaf Master in their rush through the forest.

He sat on his gigantic horse-sized toad, whose broad leathery belly inflated like a balloon with every breath. The Leaf Master smirked at them from atop the toad. The two small frogs on either side of him banged their drums rapidly.

Vidya's eyes went from one to the other, unimpressed. She wondered what type of person had the nerve to bring around their own personal drummers wherever they went. She vaguely wondered if she should make Lotus and Lily play the flute for her wherever she went, and the thought of Lotus dancing with a flute made her choke back a laugh. Looking at the Leaf Master up close, he looked less fearsome than he had been from their position watching him in the tree just a few hours ago. He certainly looked very old, from what Vidya could see of his face within the hood of his robe. His grey fur had started to go a white, almost transparent colour, and his eyes were a watery silver.

He sat in front of them, blocking their exit, surveying them one by one.

"You see," he rasped. "The explosive marshes remain asleep at night when the sun goes down and the air cools. But once the sunlight reaches them—" he gestured a claw toward the east behind him where the sky was increasingly brightening. "— They will be awoken, and a chemical reaction will take place, igniting the oily ground, and *BOOM,* everything will go."

"What do you want with us?" asked Vidya, "We're here minding our own business."

"Ah ha," chuckled the Leaf Master. "This is my domain, Fae child. Meaning, whatever goes on here *is* my business. And when I see four Fae children in my territory, I have a problem with that."

"What problem?" asked Lotus angrily, stepping forward. "Just let us go. Our business is not with you."

The Leaf Master's mouth stretched into a slow, thin smile.

"But give us back our noses first," added Willow as an afterthought.

"Ah, so you *do* want something from me," sneered the robed koala.

"Well," he spread his arms out in a grand gesture. "I am nothing if not honest. Solve my riddle, and you may be allowed out of my territory with your noses."

"*And* you will no longer terrorize the Yara-ma- yha-who," said Vidya angrily.

The Leaf Master's eyebrows flew up under his hood. He blinked, then grinned widely.

"Oh, then it will be an extra difficult one. If you cannot solve the riddle, your noses and your lives are mine. You will live here with me as my servants."

Vidya's heart sank. Perhaps she had made a mistake adding in that last part to save the Yarama. The image of the Yarama Chief mumbling into the dirt had stuck with her like a stain on her shirt, and she couldn't take it back now.

"What's the riddle then?" asked Willow nervously.

The Leaf Master, in his element, closed his eyes and spread his hands out once again and droned in a deep rumbling voice that gave Vidya the shivers.

> "I'm foolish and I'm selfish.
> I till the soil and dig the land
> And will fulfil your every wish
> All the earth I do command
> Come at me with your best
> And I'll chop you up
> Good and fresh."

The four kids and Pancake stared at him, then stared back at the lightening sky. *How long do they have?* Vidya thought. Her mind raced. This was not going to be easy. She had no idea what the answer to the riddle was. And by the looks on their stunned faces, the others didn't know either.

"By my estimate," said the Leaf Master, clasping his claws in front of him. "You have fifteen minutes."

Lotus and the others gaped at each other. Vidya turned her back on the Riddle Master and led them a few steps away, huddling the four of them and Pancake together in a circle.

"How do we get out of this?" hissed Willow. "Does anyone know the answer?"

"I say we just run," hissed Lotus. "Just bolt up into the air and shoot away above the treetops. He can clearly follow us on the ground, but'll be much faster in the sky."

Vidya nodded, considering that plan might very well work.

"But our noses," said Lily. "We need them back."

That was also a good point. If they just escaped, they would have to leave their noses behind. But if they got the riddle wrong, or didn't answer on time, everything was lost and the whole plan fell apart. Vidya imagined Lobey, the triplets, and Daisy waiting anxiously for them back home, all sitting in the library, peering out the window for any sign of their return. She imagined baby Mahiya asleep safe and sound in her cot, blissfully unaware of what her big sister was doing. Everyone was relying on them to come back and get this right. They couldn't fail, they just couldn't.

"I say we take him down," hissed Vidya. "There are five of us and four of them. We could do it."

She was met with silence.

"You mean attack him?" asked Lily incredulously. "But, Vidya—"

"I agree," said Lotus. "I think that's our way out."

"But how?" asked Willow. "He's some sort of powerful creature, that's for sure."

"Powerful or not, he looks like he can take an arrow just like any other animal," said Lotus. "Will, how many of the frogs do you think you can take out quickly?"

Willow's jaw clenched.

"There's no other way out of this, Will," she reminded him gently.

"I don't like it," he said. "But I'm quick. I can probably do them all within five seconds."

"No," Vidya shook her head, changing her mind. "I want Will to focus on the Leaf Master, since he is our best bowman. There are three of us left. Each one of us will take a frog each. I'll take the biggest."

The others nodded. Next to Willow, Vidya was the best archer.

"When I give the signal," Vidya whispered. "Take out your target. Lotus, you're the fastest on your feet, you and Will get back our noses, and we'll fly off into the sky."

"Five minutes left!" droned the Leaf Master behind them, making them all jump.

"I've put a few flowers in my bag," whispered Lily.

"And some of the oily liquid. So we don't have to worry about that."

Vidya nodded and turned, walking toward the koala. He smiled in an unkind way down at her. Vidya felt Pancake clutching at the inside of her pocket very tightly.

She cleared her throat.

"Why noses?" asked Vidya, trying to buy time.

The Leaf Master gave her a smile that said he knew exactly what she was doing. Then he tilted his chin and answered.

"I collect the noses as taxes from the Yarama. Eating Fae noses is how I've lived for so long," he pulled out a nose from his pocket and gave it an appreciative squeeze. "You can also learn a lot about a person just from their nose."

Vidya tried to make out whose nose it was, but she couldn't tell from this far. It could have been any one of theirs.

"See now, this nose, tells me this person is rather fickle minded. Always going this way or that, never in one direction." He moved the nose to his other claw and fished back into the same pocket, bringing out a slightly smaller one. His eyes met Vidya's, and he smiled at her meaningfully. "Now *this* one is a *queenly* nose, but there is something—" he shrugged, and it put the two noses back into the pocket.

"What?" blurted Vidya, thoroughly embarrassed she'd asked.

The Leaf Master's smile faded, and he regarded her seriously. "A decision must be made, Fae Queen." He abruptly turned in his saddle and pointed at the sky. "Decide on your answer, children, or into pieces you'll become."

Vidya felt everything suddenly come into sharp focus as she looked into the pink sky the same colour as her mothers' hair. The Bunyip King would launch his attack in just two nights, the night of the new moon. There was no time. She needed bring the fire flower back to the palace and bring the magic back to the Flower of Awakening. The answer came to her as quick as lightning.

"The answer to your Riddle, is *the Bunyip King*," sneered Vidya. "GO!" she screamed.

Vidya darted out of the way and drew an arrow, quickly loosening it at the huge toad. She got him right in the shoulder, and he let out a roar of pain.

The Leaf Master groaned from on top of the toad and slid off it with a thump, Willow's arrow lodged right smack bang in his shoulder. Two arrows quickly followed, Lily missed her frog, but Willow launched a second arrow, shooting through the frog's hand so he was pinned to the ground. The other smaller frog had fallen over and was now still.

Lotus' yellow form darted forward, with Willow close behind. They crouched over the Leaf Master and fished in his pocket.

"You won't get away with this…" he rasped from the ground, clutching his tummy.

Lotus held the bundle of noses in his hand and waved them at the robed koala. "Looks like we are!"

The four Fae kids leapt up into the air, wings fluttering so fast that they darted high in the sky and over the Leaf Master, directly into the sunlight over the forest.

"We'll fly as long as we can!" called Vidya once they had lost sight of the marshes. "And then—"

BOOOOOOMMM

The marshes behind them exploded in a gigantic cloud of smoke and fire, and the kids clapped their hands over their ears.

"Do you think he—" wondered Lotus.

Vidya shook her head. The Leaf Master was far too cunning and far too old to have gotten caught up in the explosion. He was safe to rule another day; she knew that much to be true.

"I can't believe we got away with that!" cried Lily.

"Me neither," admitted Vidya, shaking her head. "Here, Lotus, I want my nose back."

Lotus cackled, and they gathered in the air, looking at the noses in his hand. They were all quite similar.

"I don't want anyone else's nose," complained Lily. "Oh, that's definitely mine, it's the smoothest." She snatched it up and held it close to her chest.

"This is the biggest," pointed Pancake from Vidya's pocket. Lotus shrugged and took his.

"There's a tiny pimple on this one, it's mine," said Willow sheepishly.

Vidya took the remaining nose. They hovered in the air, staring at their noses, wondering what to do next.

"On three?" suggested Lily.

The others nodded.

"One — two — three!"

Vidya squished her nose back into the centre of her face as Pancake turned his head, watching each of them in turn. With a loud wet sound, she felt her nose suction back onto her face and suddenly; she felt cold morning air flood through her nose.

"Oh!" she said. "That feels good!"

Lily danced in the air with glee. "Does it look right?" she asked Vidya, pointing her face out in front of herself.

"Looks perfect, Lily!"

"Oh, thank the earth," sighed Willow. "This all turned out well. Imagine if—"

"Lotus!" cried Pancake. "Your's is on sideways!"

"Oh no!" yelled Lotus, panicking, pulling at his nose, trying to take it back off.

But unfortunately for him, it wouldn't budge.

SAVING THE FLOWER

"Sometimes the night seems so dark that it feels like the sun will never rise again. But all saplings know—it is in the darkness that roots grow deep. And it is only after this that the green shoots can be born, ready to meet to sun when he rises. Because he always will."

—The Book of the Fae, Queen Mab the First, 3333 B.C.

Vidya, Lotus, Willow, Lily, and Pancake flew as far as they could, northeast, in the direction of the palace, for as long as they could. The Wollemi Pine King had told them what to do to recharge the Flower of Awakening. They had the wood to make the bow and arrow, and now they had the fire flower. All they had to do was get back home and prepare the spell and then head back out to the Bunyip Nest to do it. Once their wings grew tired, they flew down into the trees and walked cautiously through the bush. Within a few hours, they were out of the forbidden zone and back into familiar territory. It felt like a weight had lifted off their shoulders, to see the familiar canopy of sprightly gum trees. But Vidya had to remind herself not to be fooled into a false sense of security. Anywhere in the Fae forest, Bunyips could be lurking, ready to attack the Fae. They had to keep their guard up at all times. But it was difficult, as they were tired, sore, and hungry. They hadn't packed near enough food and had hardly slept the last two days.

They all gave exhausted groans of relief when they saw the glint of the tall spires of the Fae palace. They had made it. Feebly, they crossed the gap over the Bottomless Sky, and the Fae children guarding the front of the palace blew their horns to announce their arrival.

Much like how Vidya had arrived back from her trip to the Old Ones just a few days ago, the four of them touched down wearily, shuffling back up to the palace, Pancake fast asleep in Vidya's pocket. A whole group of Fae kids spilled out of the large front doors and ran toward them.

"We'll have a meeting," said Vidya, waving off a worried Toad and Luna.

"What's wrong with Lotus' nose!" exclaimed Lobey.

Lotus gave a weak laugh. "It's a long story, but let us rest a moment please. We've been travelling non-stop and didn't sleep at all last night!"

The group walked together up the palace stairs and into the library, where the other kids brought out chilled glasses of orange juice and fruits and vegetables to eat. Daisy even brought out a non-burnt cake that wasn't crooked. The four kids and Pancake ate greedily as they filled everyone in on how they had travelled to the Wollemi Pine King, were captured by the Yarama, and how they battled the Leaf Master in the explosive marshes.

"The Bunyips plan to attack us on the night of the new moon, the darkest night," said Vidya. "It was lucky we overheard that conversation."

"But that's tomorrow night!" cried Luna.

"Exactly," said Vidya firmly, her hands on the table. "Now, I know we're all tired, but we have no choice. We need to execute the spell tonight." She looked around the table. "We'll sleep and wake up at dusk and head to the Bunyip nest. The rest of you prepare your weapons."

"Weapons?" asked Toad.

"Yes."

The room went silent.

"We're at war, everyone. They're coming to take away our home. There's no way around it. When we shoot. It's to kill."

"There's always been a way around it, Vidya," said Will. "Every other time in our history—"

"But this is like no other time, Will," Vidya replied, her voice rising. "When have the Fae ever had an angry army fly over across the bottomless sky to come and get us?"

No one had an answer.

"Never," urged Vidya. "This has never happened to us."

"Right," Lobey said. "We've got plenty of weapons, but we'll put everybody on alert."

"I want the young children and the babies locked away at the back of the city," said Vidya. "I want them as far away as possible from where the Bunyips are going to enter."

Lobey nodded. "I'll start the evacuation."

Vidya nodded back. "Off to bed, everyone. Willow, start on that bow and arrow as soon as you can."

* * *

That afternoon, they woke up, and Willow hurriedly began whittling away at the wood of Wollemi King, with the help of two other Fae kids. Luna and Toad were trying to fiddle with Lotus' nose, meanwhile, Vidya, Lily, and Lobey examined the black fire flowers.

"It's smells bad doesn't it?" said Lobey, holding one up. "But how do we make it light up?"

Vidya and Lily exchanged a knowing glance.

"The Leaf Master said something about how the sun would come up and activate a chemical reaction," said Lily.

"But the fire flowers the Yarama had in their little lanterns were lit up, and there was no sun in their dark village."

"How many did you bring back?" asked Lobey.

After a few hours of experimenting with the two flowers Lily had bought back, they were no closer to finding out how to activate the flower. Lily threw her hands up in the air, "I'm out of ideas."

"Vidya…" said Lobey slowly, giving Vidya a strange look.

"The Fae Queen gets certain powers, right?"

Vidya frowned for a moment. It took her a second to realise Lobey was talking about the fact she was the Fae Queen now. "Right… my father said the King or Queen has greater Fae powers… like…" a memory sparked in her mind. Her father not only had a guardian plant, but he was able to communicate with other plants as well. Not in the same way as a guardian, but enough to get by.

Vidya looked at the fire flower sitting in the palm of Lily's hand. "Fire flower, tell me how you light up."

Vidya heard nothing. She tried it a different way. "Fire flower, light up," she commanded.

The black flower shivered on the spot, then burst into a ball of yellow-orange fire. Lily screamed and dropped it. And there it sat on the grass, a tiny ball of fire.

"Well, there we go," said Lobey, clapping her hands. "Lucky you're the Queen."

Vidya only felt relief. They had it. Once Willow and the others were done with the bow and arrows, off they would go into the Bunyip's nest.

* * *

As the sun sank low in the sky, Vidya kissed baby Mahiya's forehead and passed her back to Toad. Then she, Lotus, Lily, and Willow walked out of the palace doors together. There was a tension in the air now, a heavy feeling that sat between them. Lobey had offered to change places with one of them so that Lotus or Lily could get a chance to rest and she could offer fresh energy to the task ahead. But the kids all declined, saying that the four Fae kids and Pancake knew each other well now, and all five of them wanted to finish what they had started together.

They launched themselves across the bottomless sky, the two Fae guards waving goodbye behind them. Vidya looked out over the Fae forest. It seemed darker at that moment, but no movement shifted in between the line of gum trees. She looked up at the small slither of the moon in the sky. This time tomorrow night, the Bunyips would come to stand at that same tree line before flying across the sky to find the Fae.

Right now, on Vidya's orders, Lobey and the others were moving the smallest kids to the far side of the Fae city, as far as they could get, away from the forest side. Vidya didn't want Mahiya or any of the other babies anywhere near the battle. She shuddered in the cool dusk air.

The team touched down on the other side.

"This time," Vidya said as evenly as she could. "When you shoot, shoot to kill."

The others nodded silently.

"We're ready, Vidya," said Lotus. "We'll do what we have to do."

"Then let's go."

.   .   .

Since it was dark, Willow took the lead again, followed by Lily. Together, as they branch-hopped through the forest, they checked the path ahead for Bunyips and their tracks. It was only a few minutes before they came across the first of them.

Willow raised his fist up to let the others know to stop, his body rigid with tension. He turned his face to look at Vidya, and she saw his face was ashen and taut with fear. He put a firm finger to his lips, and Vidya looked out to where he now pointed. No less than five Bunyips slinked ahead of them. Moving like sinister shadows in the dark, their fleshy grey wings flapped behind them. They were loitering in a clearing, discussing something.

Lotus fluttered silently onto Vidya's branch.

"Should we kill them?" he hissed in her ear, gripping his bow tightly.

She shook her head. It would cause a great noise to be sure, and five was too many. Vidya was just about to suggest that they fly into the air and fly to the Bunyip nest when the Bunyips in the clearing made a sudden movement, and as one group, they beat their wings and rose into the air.

"Forward!" one of them cried. And together they advanced forward in a tight unit. "Right!" the same Bunyip cried, and smoothly, they flew perfectly to the right.

"Dear mother earth," breathed Lotus. "They've been practising."

The gaping hole in the bottom of Vidya's belly grew deeper. She felt sick. They needed their parents back—

they needed their Fae magic back, and right now. She took a deep, silent breath. Willow turned on his branch, and she signalled she should go back the way they came.

Willow and Lily followed Vidya and Lotus this time, silently moving away from the practising Bunyips. Vidya led them to circle around the group to ensure they would not come close to being seen. Once they were past them and deeper in the forest, Willow took the lead again.

They passed two more groups of Bunyips practising in the forest. Each team had managed to fly in tight formations and were clearly able to use their wings now. Taking a wide berth around the groups made their trip longer, as they had to be more careful, and soon it was deep into the night, the stars twinkling above them, before they reached the Bunyip's Nest.

They were all gathered there, great, massive, heaving, black bodies, muscular and pacing, rumbling voices taking up the clearing.

The Bunyip King stood in front of his wooden throne, addressing the group, waving his massive claws in the air for silence.

"The Fae took everything from us!" cried the Bunyip King.

The Bunyips roared in agreement, and the Fae kids covered their ears.

"Now we will take it back!"

"YES!" the group cried.

"Tomorrow," said the Bunyip King quietly.

But during his speech, Vidya heard another voice.

"*Vidya....*" Came the familiar voice in her head. "*I feel you close by.*"

"*Flower of Awakening!*" Vidya said quickly in her mind. "*I'm here! I'm here to save you! I have a bow and arrow from the wood of the Wollemi King.... and a fire flower. The reaction between them should create the magic you need to recharge!*"

"*Tired...*" was all the flower said.

"*Hold on!*" Vidya cried desperately in her mind.

"Let's go while they're distracted," said Lotus, rubbing his eyes tiredly. "Let's go."

Vidya frowned at Lotus. There were deep bags under the older boy's eyes that she had not seen before. A bad feeling gnawed in the depths of Vidya's belly, and it only increased the urgency of what they were there to do.

They edged around the Bunyip Nest, closer to the entrance of the cave where the golden light now looked dangerously faint.

Before they had left, they'd decided on a simple plan. Willow, who had the least chance of getting this wrong, would shoot the fire flower into the wall of the cavern near the Flower of Awakening. Vidya would then command the fire flower to set itself alight, and then they would leave, quick smart, letting the magic do its thing.

The Bunyips seemed to all be looking right at the Bunyip King, and caught up in his moving speech, they didn't notice Willow as, crouched low, bow and arrow held at the ready with the fire flower already stuck to the tip, shot toward the cave, Vidya and Pancake close behind.

Vidya couldn't help but smile as she saw how far Willow had come. He had started off as a reluctant member of the team to becoming the very person upon whom the whole mission relied upon. And he did it with square shoulders and a set jaw.

They entered the cave, Vidya's heart pounding in her chest. She would finally get to see the Flower of Awakening in person!

The first thing Vidya saw when she entered the cave was the Flower. She sat, golden and regal, the Queen of flowers looking solemn, glowing like a softer version of the sun, wide lotus like petals delicate but strong at the same time. But she did not have more than a second to marvel at it because what they had not counted on was that there would be two Bunyips stationed inside the cave, standing guard.

Willow let out a gasp as he saw them but did not stop to think. He shot the flower arrow into the wall to the right of the Flower of Awakening, at the same time, the Bunyips let out a shout.

"Light up!" Vidya hissed to the fire flower, and it did. Bursting in a ball of red light.

The Bunyips let out a warning roar, but Willow had already begun bolting out of the cave.

Vidya spun around to follow but as she did, the Bunyips, impossibly fast, darted behind her. She made it back out of the cave but felt a painful grip around the back of her neck. She, Pancake, and one of the Bunyips tumbled together into the dirt.

"Shoot!" she heard someone cry and felt the Bunyip on top of her give a grunt and fall limp. Vidya disentangled herself from the Bunyip and leapt to her feet, just as the large group outside caught on to the commotion.

An almighty roar reached her ears as the eyes of one hundred Bunyips turned their attention upon her. Ahead, she could just make out the form of the three others in the trees, waving her on. Willow had his bow in hand as he released another arrow, hitting home on the second Bunyip close behind Vidya. She bolted, fluttering her wings rapidly crossing the dirt clearing to the trees.

She noticed what was missing a second too late.

"*Vidya!*" screamed Pancake. Vidya's heart stopped in her chest as she turned to look behind her.

She watched as a Bunyip, with one huge black claw, grabbed the tiny brown ball of fur that was Pancake from where he lay on the ground, like he was nothing but a tiny rag doll.

"*Pancake!*" she screamed back.

"We have to go!" screamed Willow, grabbing a fistful of Vidya's jacket and pulling her. "Fly, fly, fly!"

As Willow pulled Vidya into the air, tears streaming down her face, the Bunyip King roared into the night.

"Let them go! Because tomorrow night—"

The Fae children flew into the night, cold wind sweeping through them as the Bunyip King's voice hit them

"—tomorrow night, you are all *mine*."

"Pancake!" Vidya sobbed into Willow's shoulder as he held her close, practically flying the both of them. Lotus and Lily came around to help support Vidya, a flutter of yellow, orange, and navy wings surrounding her.

"He's gone," said Lotus dully. "Poor little Pancake."

17

A DARK DAY

"There is a light that exists within that Fae. It is a light that flickers within us all. And in Fae children, that light is a roaring fire, bold and booming and strong. With time, like all things, it fades. And when those embers extinguish, the light moves on to the next Fae."

—The Book of the Fae, Queen Mab the First, 3333 B.C.

Vidya sat in her parents' bedroom, rocking baby Mahiya in her arms. She felt numb. Pancake's tiny body being swept up by the Bunyips was more than she could bear. She had cried more tears that she had thought was possible. They had returned the previous night; the others carrying her in their arms together. Lobey had not asked when she met them at the door. She had seen Vidya's face and looked at each of them in turn—then her eyes had gone to Vidya's empty shirt pocket, and she had known. Silently, they'd carried Vidya up to bed, and the four of them had slept together as she cried herself to sleep. Vidya refused to believe anything bad had happened to Pancake. Something in her knew he was still alive. The light in her mind that was Pancake had not gone out. She would know it if he was gone forever. That much she was sure about.

And that night, she had a clear vision from the flower of Awakening.

"Did it work?" she asked the flower as it sat in front of her.

"I... feel something," was all the flower would say.

The vision faded, and Vidya was swept up in hours of dreamless sleep. When she got up, she went straight to her parents' room to hold Mahiya for a little while.

"Fingers crossed, Mahi," she said softly. "Mother and father will wake up soon, and father will tell us what to do about the Bunyips, and we can just go back to the way things were." She kissed Mahiya on the forehead. "Doesn't that sound good?"

Mahiya blinked up at her with wide green eyes and gurgled. Vidya grinned at her baby sister.

By her parents' bedside, she waited and waited and waited. But still her parents did not wake. As they slept on, the sinking feeling in her chest grew and grew into a dark gaping hole. As it reached midday, Vidya had to admit to herself the harsh truth. The spell given to them by the Wollemi Tree King had not worked. She saw the face of the little mushroom Lily had tripped on, the one that had told her she was no Queen and the Leaf Master's raspy voice played in her mind.

"I'm foolish and I'm selfish.
I till the soil and dig the land
And will fulfil your every wish
All the earth I do command
Come at me with your best
And I'll chop you up
Good and fresh"

The Bunyip King would pay for this, Vidya decided. In whatever way she could manage, he would pay.

A commotion outside made her stand up abruptly, clutching Mahiya to her chest.

Lobey burst into the room, red faced and panting.

"We have a problem," she said. "The twelve-year olds, Lotus and a few others. They're asleep. They won't wake up."

Vidya's heart sank even deeper into the bowels of her belly. The Flower was weakening even more, and now even the children were being affected. It would weaken until the youngest children fell asleep. Vidya was ten. She would be next.

Vidya cast another look at her parents and put down baby Mahiya in her cot with a sigh. "Show me the damage."

Lotus was fast asleep on Vidya's bed. He hadn't even woken up that morning. Luna had run around the palace and the city to do a tally and found that twenty Fae twelve and some eleven-year-olds were asleep.

"We'll have to move them all this afternoon," said Vidya. "Right to the back of the city. It's time to move my parents and Mahiya as well. Our plan didn't work."

"You tried, Vidya," said Lobey gently. "Now we have to fight."

"I know, how are the bows and arrows coming?"

"We have plenty of bows," Lobey replied, "And the kids are still whittling the arrows and dipping them in the venom. I told them not to stop. We need as many as we can get."

"We do," agreed Vidya.

"What about the nets?"

"Done, and in position."

Vidya nodded.

"Lobey, I—"

"Don't, Vidya," said Lobey, her eyes red and shining. "We're all frightened. We need our Queen to be strong. Would you speak to the little kids? I think they'd like that."

Vidya agreed, everything as they knew it was changing, and whatever tonight brought was not going to be good. If her mother were here leading the Fae city, she would make sure everyone was calm and that no one was panicking. *But your mother would have never failed*, said a dark voice in the back of her mind. *Your mother always did what she set out to do*. Vidya shook herself, pushing the thought away. *Mother always did her best, and that's all I can do as well. That's what she would want me to do.*

* * *

An hour later, Vidya, Lobey, Willow, Luna, and Toad, plus two Devil's Finger plants, carried the King and Queen and baby Mahiya out of the Palace. All morning, Lobey had directed the strong trees to carry the sleeping Fae to their hiding spot, and the royal family were the last. Vidya had been holding onto hope that they would wake, but it was finally time to admit they were still asleep and hide them away to keep them safe.

As they strode past the tree houses of the Fae city, Vidya remembered how, just before all the adults had fallen asleep, Nani had told her to help her father find a solution to the mystery of what was going on. Nani had no idea how things had come about. The Devil's Fingers trees holding Nani in her hammock would not let them move her. Deciding that the fearsome trees would guard Nani better than anyone else, they decided to let it be.

But walking past the greenhouses had reminded Vidya of something else.

"Father said that each Fae king or queen is granted another power," she said out loud.

Lobey raised her eyebrows. "I was wondering when you'd remember that one," she said smoothly. "The power to create your own plant? I've been wondering which genius King or Queen came up with the Devil's Fingers."

Vidya smirked. "And the stink flower. They had a sense of humour, didn't they?"

"Have you decided what it'll be?" Lobey asked.

The idea had been creeping in the back of her mind as soon as the Yarama chief had given their noses to the Leaf Master.

Vidya ran her hands through her magenta curls and looked at her palm. Two curly strands of pink hair had come away and were now sitting in her hand. She smiled and walked over to a patch of earth just beyond her mother's rose bushes. She crouched down and dug a small hole with one hand and lay the hairs in the ground with the other. She covered it back up, whispering exactly what she had in mind into the soil. "*Grow,*" she sung in a sweet voice. "*The Fae Queen commands you to grow exactly as asked.*"

She grinned to herself and walked back over to Lobey and the others, patiently waiting for her on the path.

"Well, are you gonna tell us?" said Lobey, frowning at the patch of soil.

"It's a surprise," grinned Vidya. "A surprise for Lotus."

The procession made their way into a back corner of the Fae city. Inside a house built inside a large Blackwood tree, a secret door led into a vast space fitted with a kitchen and many cosy beds. The Fae children sat on tiny tables and stools, eating berries and painting on leaf paper with colourful paints. If the Bunyips beat them in battle, they would have trouble finding the secret house in this tree, keeping everyone safe. Asleep, but safe.

Vidya stood in front of the Fae babies and children, their tiny wings fluttering excitedly as they laid their eyes on her silver tiara. She took it off her head and passed it to Lobey, who stepped around the room, allowing them to touch it gently, one by one. They gasped as Vidya relayed the story of how the Old Ones had made her Queen of the Fae. But at the end, Daisy's question took her by surprise.

"Are we going to die?"

The backs of Vidya's eyes burned, and ice pierced her heart. She took a deep breath to steady herself, watching a tiny boy prod her tiara with a fat finger, then giggle. She gave Daisy a small smile. "I'm not going to let that happen. We will fight."

"But the Fae do not—" she began.

"Fight, I know, little one," interrupted Vidya. "But we have no choice. The Fae children are allowed to defend ourselves."

Daisy's purple wings drooped where she sat, and Vidya's heart drooped with it.

"In a hundred years' time, the Fae will tell their kids the story of how the Fae kids saved the realm. They'll sing songs about us. Of this very day. If you're frightened or worried tonight, think about that."

Daisy's face lit up. Dimples and teeth flashed in eager smiles. 'Yes' they nodded. 'A story about us! That's so exciting.'

·   ·   ·

As the older kids left the hidey house, sealing the wooden door behind them, Willow grabbed Vidya's elbow, and she turned with a frown.

"There's *always* a choice, Vidya," he urged.

"You want me to surrender?" she asked, shocked. "To hand ourselves over. To hand *Mahiya, the children* over to *them?*"

"I made a second arrow out of the wood of the Wollemi Pine King," said Willow, his navy wings twitching anxiously. "We just have to think, there must be some other—"

"I've thought and thought and thought, Will," hissed Vidya. "This is it. If you have any ideas, let me know." And with that, she turned, spun on her heel, and stomped back up to the castle, fighting tears. Did he think she wanted this? She had no choice. None of them had any choice at all!

When she reached the back door of the castle, Lily burst through, her face ashen with fright.

"Vidya!" she cried. "Hurry! Come and see!"

Vidya and the others behind her ran to the palace entrance. Against the bright blue of the Fae sky, a thick black blob was flying toward them. With a jolt, she realised it was a Bunyip, but just a single one, and holding something brown and round high in the air.

"It's Pancake!" cried Willow.

With the cry, Vidya ran out past the doors and down the long path. The others cried for her to stop but they remained hidden behind the door. This would be the first time the others had seen a Bunyip in person. Only Willow followed Vidya at a jog, with his bow and an arrow knocked at the ready. As Vidya ran down the path, she could see that dark figures were looming on the other side of the bottomless sky. The two Fae kids guarding the lawn ran to stand behind Vidya.

As the Bunyip began his descent, Vidya could see Pancake's round form held tightly by the Bunyip's two claws. But in Pancake's hands was a small white piece of cloth, and he was waving it at Vidya.

Vidya and Willow came to a halt at the end of the path, warily watching the Bunyip who was baring his sharp yellow teeth.

"It's a peace flag," said Willow, surprised. "Are they trying to negotiate?"

The Bunyip touched down meters from the two Fae, and he set Pancake down on the ground. The tiny quokka bolted toward Vidya as fast as he could.

"Oh, Pancake!" Vidya cried, running toward him. They reached each other halfway, and Vidya scooped Pancake up and kissed him all over his face. He smelled a little bad, but she didn't care.

"Vidya!" Pancake cried, tears rolling down his face. "I thought I was dead!"

"I didn't think you were," said Vidya. "But are you okay? Did they hurt you?"

Pancake looked up at Vidya with wet eyes. "Roughed me up a little. Nothing too bad."

"I'm sorry to interrupt," muttered Willow from behind them. "But there *is* a Bunyip on our lawn."

"Right," said Pancake, shuddering, glancing at the Bunyip who was impatiently waiting just meters away. "Read this. He made me write it."

Vidya unrolled the leaf paper and read Pancake's messy handwriting.

Queen of the Fae filth. Surrender to the Bunyip King now and we shall be merciful. Do not surrender, and we will wage a war on your land like the Fae have never seen. I am giving you back this small animal as a token of my generosity.

Vidya frowned at the note.

"They want us to surrender?" asked Willow, reading over her shoulder.

But before Vidya could reply, the Bunyip interrupted in a rough, jeering voice.

"That's right," he said snapping at them. "Invite us in to take over the palace and it make it ours. And we will spare your lives."

"Are you the Bunyip King?" asked Vidya.

"No. I am his General," the Bunyip sneered. "What is your answer?"

Vidya didn't even need to think about it. She scrunched the note in her hand.

"Never."

The Bunyip General threw his head back and let out a terrifying roar. Vidya clenched her jaw, determined not to clap her hands over her ears. She did not want to look scared in front of her enemy.

"I will meet you on the battleground tonight, Fae children," he sneered. And with that, he leapt up into the sky, flapping his grey wings powerfully, gaining height more quickly than any Fae ever could, and then he was back into the Fae forest, disappearing into the shadows.

Vidya was fuming. She put Pancake on her shoulder, turned on her heel, and strode back into the palace.

Vidya lifted Pancake from her shoulder and turned him in her arms to look at her.

"War is no place for a quokka," she said gently. "You need to go to the hidey house with my parents and Mahiya."

"But I want to help!" he squeaked sadly, looking at his feet.

"You've done enough, my friend." Vidya smiled at him. "And almost died while you were at it."

Pancake nodded sadly. "Keep the children company, okay?"

She placed him on the ground, and he lumbered away. She had only just gotten him back, and now she was sending him away. It made her heart ache to look at his small form scuttling away into the palace, but it had to be done.

Lobey and the others awaited her just inside the palace entry, wide eyed.

"*That* was a Bunyip?" asked Lobey, gulping.

"Yes," said Vidya fiercely. "And tonight, we will destroy them all."

Mouths dropped around her as Vidya paced up and

down the entrance hall, talking out loud.

"Once they cross the bottomless sky tonight, they will kill us all. Our spell didn't work. The Flower of Awakening is too weak, and we have no choice."

Vidya pointed at Luna. "We'll need to collect ideas, everyone. We're going to booby trap this place to the nines."

She pointed at Lily. "Lil, collect stink flower bulbs. As many as possible. Take a few kids to help you."

Lily nodded vigorously.

Then she pointed at Lobey. "Lobelia." Lobey snapped to attention. "I want to you to release the Devil's Fingers."

"All of them?"

"Every single one."

18

WAR

Thou Fae must never harm another living being, lest it be to save that being's own life.

—The Book of the Fae, Queen Mab the First, 3333 B.C.

As the last rays of the sun disappeared for the night, in a tiny back corner of the city, behind a secret door, Toad, Luna, Daisy, and the young children huddled next to each other in a group. Daisy held Pancake in her arms, rocking him like a baby. Together, they sang old songs their parents had once sung to them.

At the front of the city, high on the roof of the palace, Vidya breathed in the night air and shivered. She stood with Lobey, Willow, Toad, Lily, and a few other Fae kids their age, all with bows slung over their shoulders. Over the past hour, they had watched the

Bunyips gather on the other side of the bottomless sky, right between the trees that lined the cliff. They were like black, writhing shadows, darkening the landscape of the once peaceful forest. The Bunyips were quiet. They made no extra noise that carried across the bottomless sky, and calmly paced the length of the cliff.

"Is everything else in place, Lobey?" asked Vidya.

"Yes."

"Are you sure?"

"Yes, Vidya."

Behind them, and spread out through the whole palace, Devil's Fingers trees strode about. Somehow, Lobey had named them all. The ones who stood at the top of the castle were the nastiest of the lot and had orders to guard each Fae child with their life. Hers, a fat sturdy black one, was called Timmy, Vidya's shorter, skinnier tree built for speed, was called Wally, and Willow's sturdy fellow was Tully.

When the first stars twinkled in the sky, Vidya turned to address the gathered Fae.

"Aim well, everyone. We don't want to run out of arrows."

"I don't feel good about this," whispered Willow. "I think I already killed one or two last night."

"Well, none of us are going to feel anything good if we're dead, either."

"This isn't like the last time," said Lobey reasonably. "Last time, the Fae adults *and* Queen of the merpeople rounded up the Bunyips and trapped them. We don't have the same ability."

"*And*," added Vidya, "they're coming after us this time. They're out to get us."

"I can't believe we're still arguing about this, to be honest," said Lobey. "We're waging war tonight." She unslung her bow from her shoulder and took out an arrow. "You don't want to die, Willow," she said fiercely. "Fight!"

The sky was a deep blue now, tiny bits of orange light just left of the sun in the west.

"Draw your bows," cried Vidya. "This is it!"

They had prepared two types of arrows. The first was poisoned with the venom of the brown snake. Any Bunyip hit with it would fall to the ground within minutes.

The second type of arrow was not sharp. The end of it was a thin round balloon of a flower that was the stink flower. If you got a bunyip in the eye, the balloon would burst, releasing the awful smelling liquid that made their eyes sting badly for hours. The Bunyips would be practically blinded for the rest of the battle.

Each entrance of the palace was booby-trapped with more stink flowers. Bunyips would not be able to get through any door without getting a face-full of the stuff.

Vidya surveyed the Bunyips on the other side. They had all taken Bilberry juice tonight, and it made Vidya's eyes super sharp. So, she didn't need Willow to tell her:

"That's him, the Bunyip King."

From out of the black shadows, a huge, dark, silky form emerged. The other Bunyips hurriedly got out of the way, bowing low as their leader came to stand at the edge of the cliff. He stood tall on his hind legs and stretched his arms lazily above him. Vidya saw rows and rows of sharp, spikey teeth glinting in the starlight. He stretched out his wings, and the grey flesh flapped like a triumphant flag.

"He thinks he's already won," murmured Lobey. Vidya felt the heat rise in her cheeks, but what emerged out of the forest behind him made her fingers tremble on her bowstring.

A gentle golden glow peeked through the trees. Rays of golden light wavered as if moving to a stride. The Flower of Awakening emerged out of the forest, carried high in the air by two Bunyips on the wide bark of a tree. She sat, a tired queen, her roots dangling over the edge of the bark.

Vidya's heart beat unevenly.

"*Vidya...*" she heard the Flower of Awakening as barely a whisper in her mind. "*I need...*"

"Oh, I'm so sorry," cried Vidya out loud. The others swivelled their heads to stare at her. "I'm sorry, Flower of Awakening!" she cried. "But the evil that took you will pay."

"Are you... talking to it?" said Lobey in surprise.

Vidya nodded. "I think... I think..." but Vidya could not say it out loud.

"Say it, Vidya," Lobey lowered her bow and turned to Vidya. "Say it out loud."

Vidya bit her lip and looked at her feet. It didn't matter now; she had failed. "She is my guardian flower." Vidya turned to the rest of them. "The Flower of Awakening is my guardian flower."

228

The mouths dropped open, eyes grew big, Willow shook his head.

"Now that is something," he murmured.

"For all the good it does now," said Vidya.

A roar pierced the air, and the Fae children turned to see the Bunyip King, his head thrown back, teeth bared at the sky, roaring into the darkest night air. The other Bunyips followed suit, and the sound rumbled toward them across the Bottomless Sky. The two Bunyips holding the Flower of Awakening laid her down on the ground.

Hearts pounding, sweat trickling down their backs, Vidya and the others drew their weapons.

"Remember," said Vidya, not moving her eyes away from the Bunyips. "They are not to get further than the palace."

As one, the Bunyips rose like a black swarm of angry bees into the sky.

"Steady," warned Vidya.

"Devil's Fingers!" cried Lobey. "Be ready!"

As the black cloud of Bunyips flocked into the sky and crossed the gap between them, Vidya's heart felt like it was going to beat right out of her chest. She blinked once, twice, then marked three Bunyips in the sky as hers. They would spread out, she assumed, with a few going for each entrance to the palace.

The Bunyips flew within range, and Willow was the first to let loose an arrow, followed quickly by the others. Vidya shot arrows in quick succession. At least five Bunyips dropped out of the sky. Lobey let out a cry of triumph.

"Go!" Vidya shouted, turning to run into the palace, the others close behind. They heard the roar of injured Bunyips dropping out of the sky, and their hearts leapt with hope.

Other Fae kids continued to shoot from the windows inside the palace. Everyone was spread out to make it as difficult as possible for the Bunyips to find them while still doing as much damage as possible from a distance.

The Fae kids ran through the palace in twos and threes, the Devil's Fingers following them close behind. The Bunyips landed on the palace roof with heavy thuds. Vidya veered into a side room with Willow, while Lobey and Lily turned into another room.

Roars announced the entrance of the Bunyips into the palace. Vidya and Willow waited in their room with Wally and Tully. The two Devil's Fingers trees stood guard between the kids and door, waiting, swaying menacingly, their gnarly, bark-hands held up in a fighting stance.

Bunyips rushed past them down the corridor, and the two kids waited for one to see them. In Vidya's mind, there were only one hundred or so Bunyips in the army. That was only one hundred well-placed arrows. Vidya kept a count in her head. At least five had fallen in the sky. That meant ninety-five to go.

A Bunyip came to a halt outside the doorway to the room she and Willow were in. He snarled, baring his teeth, and leapt forward. Wally and Tully grabbed him, and Willow loosened a stink flower arrow right into his eyes. The Bunyip screamed, but a moment later, a second and third entered. The Devil's Fingers took a Bunyip each, punching them with their strong barky arms.

"The Fae Queen is here!" roared one of them. Suddenly, ten Bunyips were clambering to get into the room, trying to claw past each other.

Willow and Vidya let loose one arrow after the other. *Six, seven, eight, nine,* counted Vidya.

Three Bunyips leapt onto Tully, and he was bitten over and over again, bark flying everywhere.

Wally was being overcome with even more Bunyips.

"Out the window!" cried Willow.

The two of them turned and ran to the window, Vidya leapt through first, into the night air, followed by Willow. They turned in the air and shot at the Bunyips, now trying to get outside the window after them, but it was a small window, and only one could get through at a time. Soon, unconscious Bunyips were hanging out the window, plugging it so the others couldn't get through. The kids turned their attentions to their surroundings.

A whoosh and burst of bright light behind her told Vidya that the Bunyips had tripped the booby-trap of flames that would stop any Bunyips from leaving the palace. The last thing Vidya wanted was Bunyips entering the Fae city and finding the secret hiding spot the babies and adults were sleeping in. They had used the last fire flower and oil from the marshes that Lily had brought back. They had dribbled a tiny line of oil all the way down the length of the back palace wall and laid the fire flower in the middle. Vidya had spoken to the Fire flower firmly, 'if any Bunyip should step onto the line of oil, she should light up immediately'. Looks like the little black flower had listened, because she heard a couple of Bunyips screaming. But the fire would not stop them from flying over, so Willow and Vidya stationed themselves next to the short wall of flames and shot any flying Bunyip immediately.

"Help!" they heard a cry, followed by another.

"It's Lobey!" Vidya said to Willow.

Willow and Vidya darted into an open window that led to an empty room. They touched down and sped out into the corridor against the second story railing, looking left and right. Down in the entrance hall, a group of perhaps twenty Bunyips were struggling against a magnificent blackwood rope net made by Lily. It was their biggest booby trap. They had lined the ropes with venom and stink flower sap and weighed down the edges with heavy rocks in the hopes that once released by Lily from the palace ceiling, it would keep the Bunyips in place. But it wasn't working. The Bunyips were flailing around, one escaped out from an edge. Willow promptly shot him in the face with a stink flower bulb.

"Shoot!" cried Lobey, running around the net, shooting at the contained Bunyips.

"I'm running out of arrows!" cried Willow.

"Timmy!" cried Lobey to the Devil's Finger tree bend her. "Deliver more arrows to Will and the queen!"

Timmy, the fat tree, stomped up the palace stairs, and the two Fae kids ran to meet him. He handed them a bunch of arrows each, and the kids loaded up the quivers on their backs.

But they were too late, because a second later, Lily let out a scream.

"Argh!!" shouted Lobey. "Run!"

The Bunyips had torn apart the net and were rising into the air, snarling, jeering faces locked on the kids.

Vidya and Willow didn't waste time. They ran back down the corridor, into the room they had come in, and flew straight out the window.

Under them, at the back palace entrance, with a last splutter, the wall of flames went out. The oil had all been burnt up. The Bunyips were free to roam the city now.

"Vidya!" screamed Willow, as out of nowhere, a Bunyip flew straight into him, grabbed him, and flew off into the night.

19

THE FINAL STAND

"The Flower of Awakening knows the Darkness like an old friend. She feels it in her roots, sees it in her mind's eye, and listens to it with her heart. And then she sings to it. And merrily, joyously, excitedly, her light glows, and the Darkness, overcome with tears, nods its weary head and retreats, admitting defeat.

—The Legend of the Flower of Awakening

Vidya immediately shot after them, a brown snake arrow knocked and ready to go. But the Bunyip was flying backward, and Vidya realised who it was as they squared off in the sky.

"Let him go, Bunyip King!" cried Vidya. Her bow quivered in her hands.

A group of Bunyips swarmed around them in a loose circle. Vidya looked around her and realised she was surrounded. The Bunyip King titled his head back and laughed.

"Do you surrender, Fae Queen?" he roared.

Vidya bit her lip hard. Willow held on to the Bunyip King's arm, which was secured firmly around his neck. His navy wings were squashed against the beast's chest, and his eyes were wide with terror. Vidya's heart beat unevenly in her chest, and her mind raced.

Was this it? Was this how it ended? Would the end of the Eastern Bushland Fae be marked by this very moment, where she surrendered to save the life of her dear friend? Willow's voice reached her mind's ear. From the day he had answered the Wollemi Pine King's question for her.

'It means to see all living things as yourself. To be Fae means to see all plants and animals and beings as one.'

A hot tear trickled down Vidya's cheek. This was wrong. It was all wrong. She looked around the at the circle of Bunyips, with their sleek black coats and sharp teeth. The raspy voice of the Leaf Master entered her mind:

"I'm foolish and I'm selfish.
I till the soil and dig the land
And will fulfil your every wish
All the earth I do command
Come at me with your best
And I'll chop you up
Good and fresh"

She went over the words in her mind over and over again, like a song she just couldn't get out of her head. *She* had been foolish and selfish. The answer to the riddle had not been Bunyip King at all, the answer to riddle had been *her*. The realisation struck like an arrow to the heart, and the backs of her eyes burned. This entire time, she had encouraged Lotus and Lobey and the others to fight back, to not only defend their home, but take down the Bunyips. She had even told that weird little mushroom in the Fae forest that's what she was going to do. There had been so much anger and fear bubbling away in her. She had just wanted to do things right. Just keep Mahiya and the other kids safe. But was she even setting a good example to Mahiya? As her older sister, as the Queen of her people, she was supposed to be showing the other kids what was right. And *none* of this was right!

How could she have missed that? The Bunyips now flying around—they were creatures of the world just like her. And just like her, made bitter and angry by a threat made to their community. She sighed and lowered her bow. She had faced more dark creatures in the last two days than she had in her entire lifetime. How could she have not understood what it meant to be Fae? Willow had been right this whole time. The Fae see all things as one. All things as themselves. As Fae Queen, she should have known that. Her parents and Nani had been teaching her the way of the Fae since she was a baby. How had everything gone so wrong? She felt like she had been struck by every arrow she had shot from her own bow tonight. Her bones ached, her wings ached. Her brain ached.

"Why are we here, Bunyip King?" she asked tiredly.

The Bunyip King bared his teeth at her.

"I seek revenge for what was done to me by the Fae. I am owed! I demand your Kingdom as my compensation."

Vidya blinked away her tears. "I understand why you want it, but—"

She was interrupted by an unexpected cry as a dozen arrows flew through the air. Two caught the Bunyip King on each leg, and he stumbled in the air. Willow broke free and shot more arrows. Bunyips fell from the sky, their wings torn, limbs punctured as Lobey and five other Fae kids had sneakily shot at them from below.

The sky-high meeting was disbanded as everyone scattered in different directions. Vidya waved at Willow, and the two of them shot down into the palace grounds, some of the other Fae kids following. The Fae kids were outmatched in the air, the Bunyip's wings were too strong, it was much better if they faced them on the ground.

They touched down upon the grass with a thud, and Vidya turned to look behind them.

No less than twenty Bunyips were running toward them.

"Run!" cried Vidya.

The group split into two. Vidya, Lobey, Willow, Lily, and few others shot down the greenhouse paths, while the other group went down into the Fae city.

Nani's triple locked greenhouse was close by.

"Let us in!" cried Lobey, banging on the door. "Let us in!"

The tree locks clicked, and the door swung open. The group rushed in, a Devil's Fingers' plant locking the door behind them.

The greenhouse seemed much bigger now that it was mostly empty. Two Devil's Fingers' trees paced up and down the greenhouse, the other two were down at the end with Nani.

"How long will it hold?" asked Lily.

"This place is a fortress," panted Vidya, wiping her forehead on her sleeve. "It was made to keep the Devil's Fingers' inside. I don't care how strong they are, it'll take them ages to get in."

"We're outmatched Vidya," said Willow. "I don't know how we're going to get out of this."

"How many do you think are left?" asked Lily.

But Vidya was barely listening. She walked down the path to see Nani, sleeping soundly on her tree hammock.

She took Nani's hand in hers, sniffing softly.

"I'm sorry, Nani," she whispered. "I think I failed us all. I made the wrong choice. But at the time, I really thought I was doing the right thing. How was I supposed to save the Fae without hurting the Bunyips? All they want is us gone altogether."

Vidya thought about the days leading up to this moment. What would the adults have done differently? *Probably a lot of things*, she thought glumly. *Probably everything.* She wondered what Nani would tell her if she were here, but she just couldn't imagine it. What was she to do? Perhaps they could all just go and hide with the children, stay safe in there while the Bunyips took over their palace. *Just give it to them?* She thought. No, she could never just give away her home to these dark creatures. The Fae Queen's job was to protect the balance, and the Bunyips winning was no balance at all.

Vidya's fingers tightened around Nani's, and something rough brushed against her fingers. Frowning, she turned Nani's hand over and unravelled her fingers. In it was a scrunched piece of paper. Vidya frowned and opened it up, reading the lines of text. The paper had been torn from a book.

Deep in the core of the earth lies a roaring fire. The Fae are made of the earth, but in their hearts, just like the earth, burns a fire-bright light.

On the top of the page, Nani had written:

Mahiya.

Vidya's mind raced.

Nani had been thinking that baby Mahiya's power *did* come from the earth. Just the deepest part, the core of molten fire. *Earth-fire.*

Then it struck her like a bolt of lightening down her spine. The image of the Flower of Awakening flashed into her mind.

"Oh, my earth!" she exclaimed, wheeling around to face the others. "It didn't work because it was the wrong type of fire!"

The others walked to toward her, confused frowns on their faces.

"What are you on about, Vidya?" asked Lobey.

"The Fae are of the earth." Vidya said. "Baby Mahiya is producing fire. Earth fire. Fire that comes from deep within the earth's core. That's what she is! She's a fire Fae. That's where her power came from! Something in the earth recognised that the Flower of Awakening needed re-charging again. And so, the new princess was born with the ability to heal her. She has exactly what we need. Earth fire!"

Willow stepped forward, excitement glowing on his face. "That was what the Wollemi Pine King was trying to tell us! He didn't know about baby Mahiya, of course, so he couldn't tell us exactly!"

"I'll be needing that second arrow, Will," said Vidya. "I'm going to get baby Mahiya."

"We're going back out there?" groaned Lily.

"Yes," nodded Vidya. "But this time, it's because we're gong to win this thing. Do you have any oil left, Lily?"

The orange-haired girl reached into her pocket. "Just a little."

"That'll do."

Vidya pocketed the tiny jar. "Let's go." She raced to the door as Lobey beckoned one of the trees to unlock it.

"I'll send out Timmy first as a distraction," said

Lobey, pointing to the fat tree. "We'll shoot from behind you."

Vidya nodded, realising that if anyone had told her, a week ago, that she would entrust Lobey with her life multiple times, she would have burst out with laughter.

Timmy pushed the door open and ran out. The waiting Bunyips roared when they saw him, and Vidya and Willow followed, bows at the ready, shooting out blindly in front of them. There were three Bunyips.

Arrows whizzed past Vidya's ear as Lobey, Lilly, and the others shot at the Bunyips. Two were down, and the third followed Vidya as she darted past the others, blinded by stink sap, out and up the path toward the city. She would have to run the length of the city, she realised, and risk exposing the secret hiding spot where the others lay. They would have to make sure they were not followed.

Vidya ran through the path, down the line of tree houses, shooting in front of her, arrows whizzing past her ear as Willow shot Bunyip after Bunyip. His aim was impeccable, but he was tired, and missing some at times. They used their wings to speed run through the city. Lobey, Lily, and the others followed, shooting this way and that.

Soon enough, they approached the end of the city where the hiding place was, right on the edge of the cloud the city rested on, near the fall to the Bottomless Sky. A swarm of Bunyips roamed the area.

"Vidya!" screamed Lobey from behind them.

"Shoot!" cried Vidya, releasing arrow upon arrow.

"I'll distract them!" cried Lobey. "Hey, losers!" she

called. "I'm the Queen of the Fae! Come and get me!" She waved at them, and the Bunyips charged at her and Lily, who screamed and shot wildly.

"Cover me, Willow!" hissed Vidya as she shot a Bunyip in the face and ducked behind him as he roared as the stink sap blinded him. They shot and ducked, scooting through the trees to the tree which held the door. Glancing behind her and seeing that Lobey had led the Bunyips away, she tapped on the door, and it glowed yellow before opening. She stepped inside and indicated Willow to stay and scout outside. He flew up to the lowest branch, crouch low, arrow knocked at the ready.

Sleepy faces met Vidya as she stepped into the room. There was a stifled cry as Toad, Luna and Pancake ran into Vidya.

"Is it over?" Toad asked, eyes shining. Baby Mahiya was in her arms.

Vidya shook her head and put her finger to her lips. "I don't have time to explain, but I need to collect fire from Mahiya." She brought out the glass jar with the oil. "A single spark should do it."

Toad frowned but looked at Mahiya. "I mean... she's been a little gassy."

"Perfect," Vidya grabbed Mahiya, and the little girl squirmed in her bundle, squealing in discomfort.

"I'm sorry, I'm sorry," whispered Vidya. "Please, Mahi, give me some fire." She lay Mahiya down in a cot and unwrapped her. "Come on, little one, get uncomfortable. Give me a spark." She held the open jar at the ready, and just as Mahi gave an almighty squeal from being put down, sparks erupted from her hands and mouth. Vidya clapped the lid of the jar down on top of one and squinted at the closed jar. The oil lit up, a powerful purple-orange fire.

"Woah!" exclaimed Luna and Toad.

"Gotta go!" cried Vidya, hastily bundling Mahiya back up and shoving her into Toad's arms. She patted Pancake on the head and rushed back to the door, cracking it open and whistling. Willow jumped down and pulled the door open.

"It's clear," he said, and together, they shut the door and ran back down the path. "I hope Lobey's okay," he panted as they raced back through the city. They shot two Bunyips on the way back before they saw Lobey in the distance, racing up to the palace as a gang of Bunyips followed her.

"No time to help them," Vidya said. "We have to do this now."

"Agreed," said Willow. "Once your father and the adults wake up, we'll have triple the amount of Fae to help fight."

They half flew half ran up the path to the palace and shot up to the roof where their night had started.

Willow and Vidya ran to the edge of the roof palace, looking at the pale glow of the Flower of Awakening sitting in front of the trees.

"How are we going to create a light bright enough?" asked Willow hurriedly, glancing behind them.

Vidya licked her lips. It was risky, but it was the best idea they had.

"It'll take both of us, Will," said Vidya. "I have a little

oil left from the western marshes. I'm shooting the Wollemi arrow lit with Mahiya's fire. And you're going to take an arrow with a balloon filled with oil. We're each going to shoot an arrow, and they'll meet in the sky, creating the explosion."

Willow looked at her in surprise. "But, Vidya, the odds of us getting that right are…"

"Slim, I know. Let's go."

"We only have the one shot."

"I know."

Willow emptied a stink sap bulb of its contents, and Vidya dribbled some oil into the empty bulb. Willow carefully tied it back up.

They flew into the dark sky and crossed the gap toward the Fae forest. Two black blurs shot out of the forest, and before Vidya could react, Willow had shot two arrows, Vidya watched as two Bunyips went tumbling down into the Bottomless Sky.

"Should've known they'd keep a guard," he called.

They were tired and making mistakes now. It was lucky Willow was fast.

"Thanks, Will," was all she could say.

She glanced down at the Flower of Awakening, who glowed so weakly, she was barely glowing at all. She nodded at Will, and they spread out in the sky in front of her. If all went well, they were going to meet their arrows right in front of the flower.

The Bilberry juice was fading, so Vidya could barely see Willow out there in the dark. But this was the best she had. She took a deep breath, took a clean arrow, and dipped it into the jar full of oil and Mahiya's fire.

The arrow lit up, and she dropped the jar into her backpack.

Vidya knocked the flaming arrow and pictured the Flower of Awakening in her mind. Willow aimed his arrow.

"Go!" he shouted.

Vidya shot hers into the air, and half a second later, Willow shot his. And true to his aim, the two arrows met in the night air.

* * *

Lobey and Lily ran into the palace, over ten Bunyips on their tail. Their best bet was battling them in a confined space, she decided. Three Fae kids waited for them in the small back door they were heading through, in the process of pushing a heavy wardrobe across the door.

"Barricade the door!" cried Lobey, darting through after Lily.

They heaved the wardrobe into place as the Bunyips made it to the door, shoving and pushing at it while the Fae kids pushed with all their might from the other side to keep it in place.

Lobey checked the entrance hall and saw a Bunyip was crouched on the floor, an arrow in either leg. It was the Bunyip King, injured and faint. Another large Bunyip lay on the floor next to him. Was this it? Had they won? But a roar reminded her that ten more perfectly healthy Bunyips were trying to get through the back door. It didn't matter that their King was injured.

Lobey reached into her quiver and found it empty. Her heart fell. She was out of arrows. She spun around, looking for her options as the Bunyips smashed the wardrobe from the other side. A broken cupboard sat against the wall, nothing more. She turned to Lily who looked back at her, dirty faced, torn clothed, and tear streaked, panting. Her quiver was also empty. The wardrobe burst and splintered to pieces.

* * *

BOOM!

A ball of purply orange flame blared into the night sky, making Vidya and Willow cover their eyes. As the light dimmed, Vidya looked around.

The molten light dispersed in the sky, but it didn't fade away. Strangely, it hovered in the air, glowing above the two Fae children. Something was holding it in place. Vidya looked around to the Flower of Awakening.

Beams of purple and orange light were streaming toward the flower. She was drawing the light in like she was drinking water, her petals gleaming brighter with every second that passed.

Vidya grinned at Willow.

* * *

The Bunyip King froze on his spot on the palace floor. Like a jolt of lightning, a great pain pierced through his body. It hit him in the brain first, then shot down into his heart and belly. It was an awful, stinging sensation.

On his knees, eyes screwed shut, he came to the stark realisation of what the pain was. The word came to him, matching the sick feeling in his stomach.

Guilt.

He opened his eyes and looked up from the floor.

Around him, the Fae palace was in tatters. Tiles were cracked, walls were covered in dirt and ash. Two Fae children clung to each other toward the side of the entrance hall, one with electric blue hair and the other with orange. They were crying. Three other Fae children were cowering in the corner, screaming. His army poured through an open door, stepping over the shattered pieces of a large... *wardrobe*. How did he know that word?

He had done this. He was responsible for these children's pain. He was responsible for the destruction of the palace. The shock of his new emotions made him tremble on the spot. The backs of his eyes burned. Why was that? Hot liquid seeped out of his eyes and down his cheek. He raised a large claw to his face and wiped it, then examined his claw. As his throat tightened, he knew the word for what the clear liquid was. *Tears*. To his right, his General rolled around the floor, legs and arms curled in tight. A high-pitched rumble was coming from him, and with a jolt, the Bunyip King realised his General was sobbing. Further up the stairs, another one of the Bunyips was standing as still as a tree, peering around the palace in confusion. A whole swarm of his Bunyips lumbered slowly toward him, their faces contorted with fear and confusion. They looked around their surroundings with wide eyes.

The Bunyip King suddenly understood what he had to do. He cleared his throat.

"Retreat!" he roared, his voice not sounding like it was his own. He cleared his throat again. "You all!" he pointed a claw at the Bunyips now gathering in front him. "Spread the word, gather the others, the Bunyips are to retreat!"

REUNION

For even the darkest of creatures, when given the light, will choose it, every single time.

—The Book of the Fae, Queen Mab the First, 3333 B.C.

Behind the secret door in his hiding spot, King Farrion was the first to awaken. He sat up bolt upright.

"Vidya!" he cried.

He was met by a red faced Linaria holding baby Mahiya, and Pancake held by Daisy.

"Toad?" he said, looking around him at the Fae children gathered there, confused. "Luna? Daisy?"

"Uncle!" Toad cried,

"Aunty!" cried Luna, looking past him.

King Farrion shot a look to his left and saw the

Queen was stirring in her sleep, blinking her eyes open. He looked around at the stirring adult Fae, all carefully placed on beds, then he looked to his right and saw tiny children and infants, sleeping together in cots. He understood immediately.

"Tell me everything, Toad," he commanded.

The adults woke up around them as Toad, Luna, and Pancake explained what had happened. Farrion and Salote, now awake, calmed everybody down before Farrion the adults and an excited Lotus prepared to step outside the hidden house and see what had become of the war. Farrion had just put his hand on the door handle when someone knocked on it from the other side and turned the handle.

Farrion pulled the door open and Vidya, Willow, Lobey, Lily and a whole bunch of bruised and dirty Fae kids fell through the door.

"Oh, mother earth!" came a cry.

"You won't believe it!" said another.

Farrion pulled Vidya to her feet. "What's going on Vidya?"

"We fixed it!" cried Lobey, jumping up in the air. The other kids cheered and ran into the room looking for their parents. There were cries and happy tears. Daisy showed her parents one of her cakes, and Toad passed baby Mahiya back over to the Queen. Lotus hugged Willow and Lily, grumbling how he'd missed everything. Vidya grabbed Pancake and swung him through the air.

"It's over, father!" she laughed. She set Pancake on her shoulder and rubbed her eyes, explaining how she and Willow re-energised the Flower of Awakening and restored the Fae magic. Lobey explained how just as the Bunyips were about to win the battle, everything changed.

"And then the Bunyips just... stopped!" exclaimed Lobey, who was hugging her parents and sisters. "They stopped attacking us and just stared around like they were confused by the whole thing. And the Bunyip King said to me, *'I'm sorry.'* Can you imagine? The Bunyip King said *that* to me!"

Vidya laughed as she went over to hug her mother. "Looks like the Flower of Awakening evolves creatures. It makes them wiser. So, when we gave the Flower a boost of power, the Bunyips got a boost of the magic as well. And now, they don't want war with us. They just.... well... I'll let you see for yourself."

King Farrion and Queen Salote exchanged a look.

"Where is your Nani?" asked the Queen.

"She's already out inspecting the grounds," said Lobey, disentangling herself from her mother. "There are a lot of Devil's Finger trees that are injured from the battle. She and I will have to work to patch them up." The adults gave her a quizzical look, which Lobey had been waiting for. "Oh," she shrugged. "They're my guardian plant." Her parents exclaimed, and the adults shook their heads and smiled, but then Lobey gasped in remembrance. "But you'll *never guess* what Vidya's guardian plant is!"

The Queen laughed and hugged Vidya tightly. "I'm so happy for you Vidya! What is it?"

Vidya looked around at the Fae kids. The Flower of

Awakening had been a myth just a couple of days ago. "I think it's best I show you instead. And Bunyips are gathered on the front lawn," Vidya grinned at Willow. "They're a little confused by the whole thing. We should go speak to them."

They left the hidey house as a big group and made their way back up to the palace. They passed Nani directing Devil's Finger trees to walk in single file back to their greenhouse. She came over to join them as they passed and put her arms around Vidya's shoulders.

"I'm so proud you figured it out," she said happily. "It's such a shame I wasn't there to see it!"

"Lucky I came across that paper in your hand, Nani," said Vidya. "It was a close one, that's for sure."

On the way to the palace, the Queen did a tally of who was present. Everyone had been accounted for except Uncle Billy, the King's bachelor brother, who had been known to go adventuring into the Fae forest alone.

"We'll find him, Vidya," said her father reassuringly. "He's probably lost in the forest somewhere."

Vidya nodded tiredly and everyone, the triplets, Daisy, Lotus, Lily, and Willow, all with their parents, gathered on the front lawn just outside the palace entrance, watching the scene before them. Vidya's parents moved to the front of the group.

The Bunyips sat in a great huddle on the front lawn, the Flower of Awakening sat in their centre. They all gazed toward the great golden flower, who now shone with such brilliant gold light that it was impossible to look at her directly for too long. The Bunyips were muttering to one another, discussing the night's events. Vidya explained that their arrows had done little to permanently injure any of the Bunyips, the brown snake venom and the stink flower sap had very temporary effects on the tough creatures.

King Farrion surveyed them from the side. The Bunyip King, feeling that he was being watched, looked up to meet the eyes of the Fae king. He rose from his seated position and strode through his people over to the King.

"Fae King," rumbled the Bunyip King.

"Bunyip King," said King Farrion.

"I believe I owe you an apology. I will prepare a formal speech to apologise to your people."

King Farrion was not entirely sure what to say to this, but he was King after all, so he went for honesty instead.

"This is most unexpected."

The Bunyip King cocked his head. "It is," he agreed lightly.

The sky brightened in the east, and the two Kings looked over at the canopy of the Fae forest. Pink and orange streaks of light spread across the sky, followed by the tip of the orb that was the dawn sun. The light hit the palace wall first, and as the sun rose into the sky, the light fell upon the palace grounds. Sparks flew from all around them as the magic of the Fae shot out of the trees, the bushes, the plants and even the grass. The sun fell upon the Flower of Awakening sitting in the centre of the group of Bunyips and the closest gasped as a beam of light shot out of the centre of the golden flower. A magic wind whipped through the lawn, and the plants bounced and flurried, leaves rustled in a dancing display of the Fae magic.

All over the Fae city, plants shot up and grew meters taller, flowers bloomed, fruits ripened, berries grew sweet, and vegetables plopped out of the earth. Fae all over the palace cheered and clapped their hands. The dawn of spring had come, the power of Fae magic had returned stronger than before.

Vidya turned and grabbed Daisy, standing with her mother behind them, eyes wide. "Dance with me, Daisy!" cried Vidya, and the two girls twirled around in the dawn sun, giggling.

As they came to a halt, Daisy dizzy with the dance, Vidya gasped at a memory. She turned on her heel, running through the palace and out the back, down the garden path that led to the city. Halfway down, she skidded to a stop. A group of Fae had gathered around a large, glowing tree. There, from the hair she had buried in the soil just yesterday, now stood a beautiful tree laden with… Vidya squinted at the brown-coloured fruits that were growing from the flowers on the thick branches.

"Is that a… nose?" asked someone incredulously.

"Dear mother earth," gasped another. "That's a nose! And there's another nose!"

Vidya could not help herself. The relief of her parents waking up, the Bunyips stopping the war, and now the picture she'd had in her mind's eye become real… she let out a cackle of wild laughter. A Fae baby saw her from his father's arms and also began chuckling, and soon everyone gathered around the tree was laughing at what they were seeing.

"What's going on?" came her mother's voice from behind her. Vidya turned and saw her mother carrying baby Mahiya, squinting at the new tree. Vidya pointed at the nose 'fruits'.

"They're… They're noses," she said through laughter. "I-I grew it myself, as my Queen's plant, after Lotus' nose couldn't be fixed, I wanted to grow him a new one!"

Queen Salote chuckled. "My, what a great use for a tree, Vidya. The Yarama will be jealous."

Vidya wiped a happy tear from the side of her eye, nodding. "Yes, that was another thought I had."

"Do you think…" said a wispy voice from behind them.

Princess Vidya and Queen Salote whirled around to find Uncle Jula-wil hobbling up to them, cane in hand, eye patches in place. He pointed to the tree with his cane. "Do you think this tree will grow eyeballs?"

Vidya smiled, "Oh yes, most definitely, it should grow new eyes for you, Uncle Jula-wil!"

"Oh no," said the elderly echidna waving his stick. "The eyes are not for *me*." And he pivoted to the right and strode right into the rose bushes.

Queen Salote shook her head at him, the expression on her face made Vidya giggle.

"Come on, love," she said, turning to walk back up to the palace. "I believe we have some decisions to make."

They joined King Farrion and the Bunyip King out on the front lawn once again.

"Vidya," said her father, beckoning her over. "We have an idea, come and hear this."

The Bunyip King lifted his now-wiser brown eyes to Vidya's green ones. "The Fae King has proposed that the Bunyips become the protectors of the Flower of Awakening. She prefers equal parts sunlight and sea water. Since the Bunyips are both land and water creatures, we are well suited to the task."

"I have allocated them their own land in the Fae forest with a Fae pond," explained Farrion. "To call home and live their lives. How does that sound?"

"As long as I can see her every day, that sounds brilliant!" said Vidya.

"Well…" said the Bunyip King. "There has been developments in that area." He pointed to the bottom of the gigantic golden flower where three miniature flowers had sprouted beneath the outer petals.

Vidya gasped.

"I do not think you will ever have a problem with the Fae magic ever again," said the Bunyip King. "Princess Vidya can even have her own flower."

Vidya screamed with a happiness she had never known. It took her by such surprise that she flung herself at the Bunyip King, throwing her arms around him in a gigantic hug. The Bunyip King, startled, stumbled back a step before he blinked once, then let out a loud laugh, patting Vidya's back gently.

* * *

The next day, the King held a ceremony on the front lawn of the castle. The Bunyips were there, standing next to the excited Fae citizens. They watched on with wide eyes and wings twitching with interest, as, standing on a broad platform, the Bunyip King gave an honest speech about how he had thought he had been doing the right thing, but now, with the help of the Flower of Awakening he only wanted a life of peace. He and his people would help to repair the palace and any damage they had done.

The crowd cheered, and the Bunyip King twitched in surprise and gave them all a toothy smile before lumbering away back into the crowd.

King Farrion and Queen Salote gave their own joint speech, praising the Bunyip King for his newfound wisdom, and announced their forgiveness and excitement at a new partnership for the future.

Next, Vidya, with Pancake by her side, presented her parents with her Queen's tiara.

Her father took it with gentle hands, bowing. "You have been a worthy Queen, my daughter, and took care of our land with honour and bravery. We will hold your crown in safe keeping until your official coronation day, which is hopefully many, many, years away."

The crowd tittered and smiled at their Princess.

"In its place, we award you with this medal," the King held up a shining gold and silver medal hanging from a pink ribbon. "Princess Vidya, we award you with the Medal of Excellence for your bravery, skill, and perseverance in healing the flower of awakening and leading your people well."

Vidya bowed her head, and her father hung the medal around her neck, she grinned at her parents, who smiled proudly at her in return.

"And now," announced the Queen, holding baby Mahiya. "We ask the children of the Fae to come forward."

The triplets, Willow, Lotus, Lily, Daisy, and all the other Fae kids who fought in the battle or helped in any way, stepping in front of the adults, looking up at the royal family.

"Never in the history have we seen something like this happen. And never have the Fae seen such bravery. Each and every one of you will be awarded the Order of Fae."

The crowd cheered and clapped loudly, and the children hugged each other. The Order of the Fae was given only to the bravest of Fae, whose great deeds won them the respect and praise of the entire country. Their story would be told for many years to come.

The Queen spoke again. "Princess Vidya will now announce her awards."

"In the last few days, I learned what it means to be Fae," said Vidya, stepping forward with six gleaming gold medals swinging from her arm. The backs of her eyes stung as she addressed her friends and their parents, but she cleared her throat and continued. "We had it wrong to start with. I was angry and scared. I wanted to wage war, to fight and protect what I thought was ours. In the midst of battle, I realised that it wasn't right. Willow had been right all along. The Fae are one with the land its creatures. And where there is a smarter, kinder solution, that's the one we should always follow."

Lotus and Willow hugged and cheered at Willow's name. His parents cried happy tears in the crowd.

"To Willow, I award this Medal of Honour, for never swaying from Fae values, and teaching me the meaning of the Fae."

Willow came up, and Vidya hung the medal around his neck and hugged him. He came to stand next to her.

"To Lotus and Lily, I award these Medals of Bravery for standing by my side in the Fae forest time and time again. I will never forget it."

Lotus bounded forward, followed by Lily, and Vidya placed the medals around their necks, and they stood hand in hand with Willow by her side.

"To Lunaria and Linaria, or Toad, I award these Medals of Leadership and Compassion. Without you, the Fae palace would be in tatters and the children walking around unwashed. You led the Fae children while I was in the Fae forest."

The blue haired girls jumped up to collect their medals, coming to stand next to the other kids.

She looked at Lobey, who stood on the grass, wringing her hands nervously. Vidya grinned.

"To Lobelia, I award the Medal of Nobility, not only

for your leadership, but for saving my life with little regard for your own. You are the only Fae child known to have single-handedly crossed the bottomless sky into the Fae forest and pull me out of the frozen Fae pond, while the Bunyips were prowling close by. Without you, I would not be standing here. I owe you my life, Lobey."

Lobey, tears streaming down her face, ran up onto the platform and threw her hands around Vidya, who giggled. Vidya placed the medal around Lobey's neck.

"And lastly," grinned Vidya grabbing Pancake and making him stand in front of her. "I award Pancake the Medal of Honour because through fear, peril and almost certain death, you never ever, failed to stand beside me." She lowered her voice to a whisper so only he could hear. "Or sit in my pocket."

Pancake wept as he accepted his Medal and he and the seven Fae kids stood on the platform as everyone, including the Bunyips, cheered and whistled for them.

There was a great feast that night. The Bunyips joined in, eating all the Fae foods they had never tried before. They gasped and exclaimed, trying delicious cakes and soups and fruits. And after they ate, there was a great dance where the Fae taught the Bunyips to move their clawed feet as graciously as they could. They laughed and danced and ate the night away.

Vidya and Pancake sat cross-legged by the Flower of Awakening most of the night, writing letters to

Princess Sonakshi and Meera and enjoying a long, overdue conversation. The Flower thanked her profusely.

"You have risked your life and done so for me, Vidya," the Flower said gratefully. *"And now, I have a gift for you too."*

"Really?" asked Vidya excitedly. "What is it?"

"If you collect the nectar from my flower and drink it. It will allow you inside a person's mind, to know their thoughts."

Vidya's mouth dropped open. "You're kidding."

The Flower of Awakening, the Phoenix flower, bristled happily, her petals purring like cat.

"Nope, no kidding here."

* * *

A week later, Princess Vidya with Pancake, King Farrion, Willow, Lotus, Lily, Lobey, and the Fae guard stomped through the deepest part of the Fae forest right up to the home of the Yara-ma-yha-who tribe that had held them captive.

"Leaf Master!" called Vidya loudly. "I have a gift for you!"

It didn't take long for the *boom bump boom* of the frog's drums to start up. The two large green frogs entered first, with bandages around their limbs. Despite their injuries, they still sat on the dirt, drumming away, eyeing Vidya and the children suspiciously. Then the Leaf Master appeared on his toad steed, apparently all healed of his injuries, furry face suspicious under the hood of his black robe. He steered his toad to come and stand a healthy distance away.

"On the one hand, Princess, I am surprised to find you alive," he said in his raspy voice. "On the other hand, I am hoping you are not here to shoot me again."

Vidya gave him a mocking curtsey. "I admit I got your riddle entirely wrong. You meant *me* as the answer, didn't you?"

The Leaf Master swept her an equally mocking bow. "Indeed, it was a good little trick, wasn't it?"

"In the end," said Vidya. "You were actually the one who made me realise what I was doing was wrong. So, I have actually come to thank you."

The smile fell from koala's face, and the corners of his mouth turned down.

"Any help given was by accident, I assure you."

"Oh, I know," said Vidya lightly. "But in any case, we are here to apologise. The Fae children have recognised the error of our ways... on the condition that you recognise the error of *your* ways."

The Leaf Master sneered at King Farrion.

"Interesting child you have brought up, King of the Fae."

Farrion smirked at the Leaf Master, and Vidya stepped forward with the tree cutting they had planted in a large pot. She placed it on the ground between them and returned to stand next to her father.

"Indeed, I have, Master Koala. She has come up with a fine solution for your little tax issue."

The Leaf Master looked sharply at the potted plant. "What is that fruit tree?"

"I call it the Riddle tree," said Vidya, pointing at the small button nose hanging from the tree.

"You gave me the idea, of course. With my Queen's right, I grew a plant of my own imagination. It grows noses for you. Boogers and all, I'm guessing."

The Leaf Master's eyes widened. "What a thing…"

"Indeed," said Farrion. "You are granted the use of this plant to keep you fed, on the condition that you do not terrorise the Yara-ma-yha-who or any other creature here."

The Leaf Master's silvery-grey face surveyed the Fae in front of him.

"Is that a deal?" asked Vidya with a polite smile.

The Leaf Master nodded. "It is."

He slid off his toad and with surprising deftness for someone so round and big, snatched up the potted plant and leapt back up onto his toad. Without another word, they hopped back into the shadows of the deep forest.

"Charming fellow," commented Farrion.

"You have no idea," murmured Vidya.

Next, the troupe travelled through the clean green lawn of the home of the Wollemi Pine King and his cassowary guard.

This time, they took a petal of the Flower of Awakening as a gift.

"Oh," whispered Akurra, her bird eyes reflecting the

golden light. "His highness will be very happy with this."

Vidya, Lobey, Lotus, Lily, and Willow spoke with Tree King for hours, relaying the story of how the Fae children fixed the Flower of Awakening and battled the Bunyip army. The Wollemi Pine was delighted to hear such a grand story, 'ohing' and 'aahing' at all the right parts.

"I remembered something you said when we were here last," said Vidya at the end. "What was the other name for the Flower of Awakening? The name you said you knew her by?"

"The Phoenix flower," said the King fondly. *"That is the name we give to fire that comes from within the earth."*

Vidya explained baby Mahiya's fire powers.

"Ah," said the King. "The flower called upon her to be born when she felt her power wane. She knew what she needed, even if she couldn't say it. Princess Mahiya will be called a Phoenix Fae."

King Farrion and Princess Vidya left the Wollemi Pine King with smiles on their faces.

"Another mystery solved," mused the King.

"Too right," said Vidya. "I've had enough mysteries to last me a lifetime."

King Farrion smiled knowingly at his daughter. "When you are Queen, there'll always be one mystery or another."

Vidya smiled thoughtfully. "Well, it seems to me if I solved *this* problem, I can basically solve anything."

Then she and Pancake ran toward Lobey, Willow, Lotus (with his new nose), and Lily and together, they laughed and danced their way back to the palace thoroughly happy that they would never have to set foot in that part of the forest ever again, and even if they did, they wouldn't have a problem with it because they were Fae and whatever difficulty they faced, they'd be able to sort it out together.

AFTERWORD

I hope you enjoyed Book 2 of the Pacific Princesses Series.

Authors love to hear from readers, it's what keeps us going! Please leave an honest review of your favourite books wherever you purchased them.

Not only do authors want to see what they're doing well, or not so well, but it's the single best way to let other readers know they should read a book!

Pretty please leave a review for this book wherever you purchased it. Or send your review/thoughts to me at ektaa.bali@gmail.com, I would love to hear from you!

For exclusive sneak peaks and updates sign up to the Pacific Princesses mailing list at pacificprincesses.com and follow the facebook page at facebook.com/pacificprincesses.

ACKNOWLEDGMENTS

My heartfelt thanks to my mum, Shobna and my cousin Rachna for their tireless and tactful constructive criticism, which allowed me to make this story so much better while still preserving my feelings.

A sincere thank you to Marnie for her wonderful editing and super kind words of encouragement.

Thank you to Adrian once again, for his beautiful illustration of Princess Vidya and the Flower of Awakening for the cover.

And lastly, thank you to my niece Vidya, for being my inspiration for this story.

EXCLUSIVE PREVIEW OF THE
MERMAID PRINCESS

Read on for a sneak peak of Meera's story!

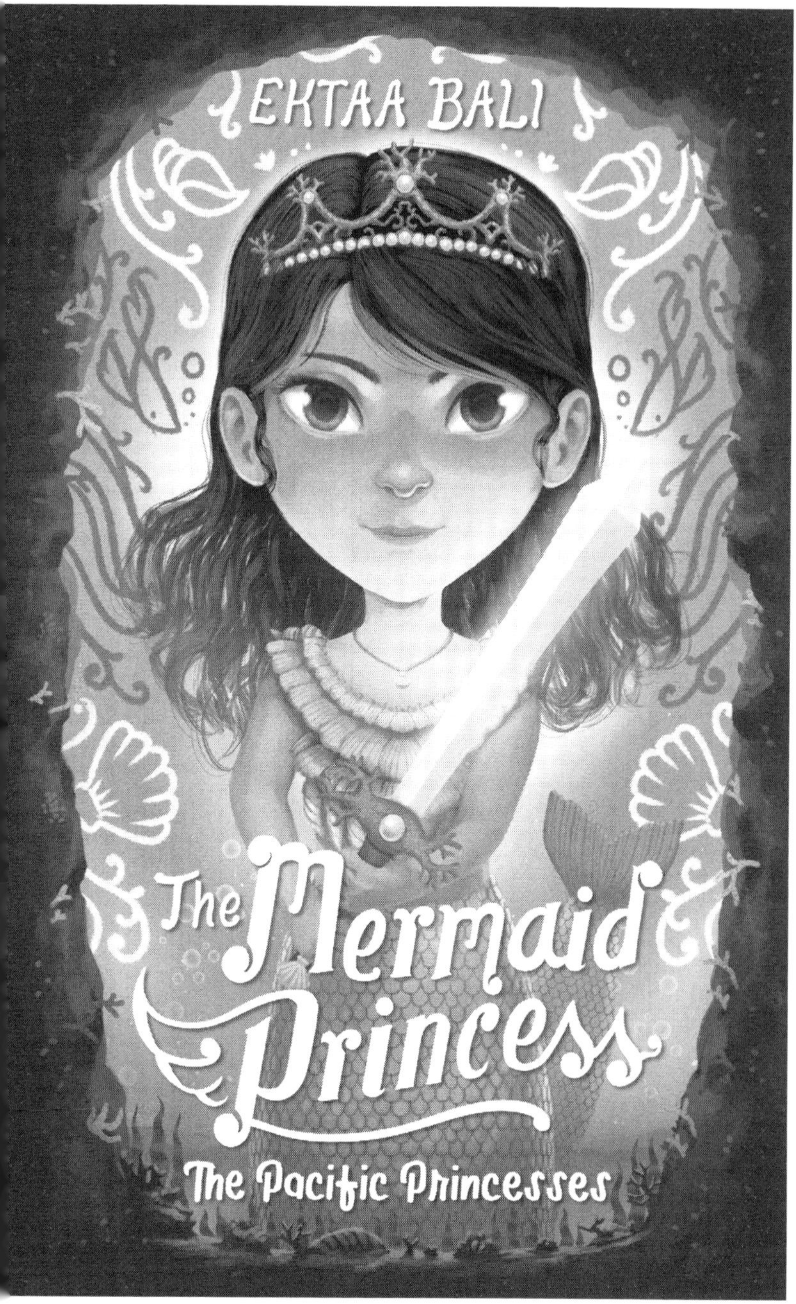
EKTAA BALI
The Mermaid Princess
The Pacific Princesses

THE BOOK OF WATER

At the dawn of time, the entire earth was one ocean. Merfolk swam throughout the seas, wild and strong. When land rose above the sea, the people of the ocean heard the call of the land. Their hearts began to glow. Those whose heart belonged to the land grew legs and left the sea to become humans. Those whose hearts were loyal to the sea remained there, holding the ancient knowledge, the ancient power, and the ancient magic. When the humans built their boats and began sailing across their old home, the Merfolk remembered them and protected their cousins from the perils of the wild ocean. Even when the humans forgot them, the Merfolk, with their long memories and wild hearts, did, and will not ever, forget.

Six mermaid queens met at a Fae pond under the light of a full moon. They sat on thrones of glass and silver built in a circle around the pond by old Mer-Kings thousands of years ago. A warm breeze tickled the leaves of the surrounding forest as each queen sat proudly, holding a brilliant trident that glittered by the magical blue-green glow of the Fae pond.

Queen Aphritie of the Atlantic Ocean held her Trident of Opal,

Queen Lorelai of the Arctic Ocean held her Trident of Sapphire

Queen Salila of the Indian Ocean held her Trident of Emerald

Queen Marea of the Southern Ocean held her Trident of Topaz

Queen Iara of the North Pacific Ocean held her Trident of Amethyst

And finally, Queen Tahlia of the South Pacific held her Trident of Ruby

But the seventh trident, the Empress Trident, was not present. It had been missing for hundreds of years and nobody had any clue where it was. The mermaid who wielded that Trident became empress of the entire ocean. And it was for this very fact that the mermaid queens met once every ten years.

Queen Aphritie raised her Opal Trident. "My sister-queens, we meet at queen's pond as our ancestors before us have done for thousands of years."

The other five queens nodded and smiled at one another.

Fae ponds are created by the combined magic of the Fae and the Merfolk. They are portals between the ocean and the land, allowing Merfolk to meet with their Fae friends whenever they needed to.

But the queen's pond was the only Fae pond of its kind, because it was six Fae ponds meeting together. It allowed the mermaid queen from each of the world's oceans to meet at one place without having to swim hundreds of kilometres.

"As the old queens swore a vow to keep peace in the six oceans," said Queen Lorelai. "So will we."

"So will we," murmured the others.

But what none of the queens saw, was that a seventh person had come to the meeting. Hiding in the shadows of the tall Fae trees, he watched and listened.

"Do you have the pearls, Queen Salila?" asked Queen Marea.

"I have them." The honey-skinned Queen Salila threw six shiny objects into the air. They caught the light of the moon as they flew toward each of the other five queens.

A cold wind whipped through the air, and Queen Tahlia shivered and gripped her Ruby Trident more tightly, rubbing a hand over her rounded pregnant belly as the baby mermaid inside her kicked a little too excitedly. She raised her hand and caught the pearl as it soared toward her, opening her palm to reveal the beautiful round gem of the sea set on a silver thread she could wear around her wrist.

"We bind our oaths to these pearls," said Queen Salila in a serious voice. "May they carry the light of our oaths to keep the peace. And should any of my sisters carry greed for more power in their hearts, may these pearls darken and alert us of the broken oath."

Tahlia nodded. If any one of them went against their oath and sought to claim more than their share of the ocean, the pearls would turn to black, and they would all know that one among them had betrayed the rest.

"Let us take our oaths now," said Queen Aphritie.

And so, one by one, each mermaid queen swore her oath. After Queen Iara took her oath, it was Tahlia's tun. She held the pearl in one hand and her Ruby Trident in the other.

"I, Queen Tahlia of the Southern Pacific Ocean, swear, under the light of the full moon, to rule over my own realm wisely and never seek the power of the Empress Trident of Gold."

The mermaid queens smiled at each other. They were bound as one now, and as long as each of them kept their word, there would be peace in the ocean. Each one of them would rule their ocean realm wisely and never seek to invade another's waters.

But what the queens had not seen was that a fragment of Queen Salila's pearl had chipped off and rolled into the forest behind her. She had frowned at the pearl in her hand, but then shrugged to herself. Despite its missing chunk, it was still beautiful.

The shadow in the forest hobbled behind her glass throne and, leaning on his walking stick, snatched up the small broken-off piece. He clutched it greedily and smiled an evil smile. He now held the newly made seventh pearl in his dirt covered palm.

After the sixth queen had taken her oath, the shadow watched the queens stare at their pearls expectantly.

The shadow looked down at his tiny pearl and, knowing the ways of old magic as taught to him by his sister, Mankini, he whispered.

"I, Magnot, King of nothing, swear to never seek more power than I already have."

As soon as Magnot finished the words, the Queens gasped in surprise as the six pearls lit up with a golden glow. Magnot closed his fingers over his own pearl, hiding its light from view.

The spell was complete. The oath was made.

From the darkness, Magnot smiled. The vow meant nothing to him. And it meant everything.

The six queens bade each other goodbye and slipped from their thrones back into the blue Fae pond, swimming back to their own oceans. Magnot watched them leave in a flurry of splashing water and glittering tails, and then he turned away, hobbling on his crooked legs back into the Fae forest.

But he was not watching where he was going.

Something hard thumped into him, and he fell backward onto the damp leaf litter of the forest floor, his walking stick flying out of his hand.

"Oof!" he groaned. "Who's there?" With great difficulty, he heaved himself onto his knees and felt around in the dirt for his walking stick.

The glowing orange light of a lantern swung above him, and he looked up and saw the illuminated face of a large Fae man with a blue beard. In one hand he held a sharp-looking spear.

"What are you doing here, Magnot?" asked King Farrion of the Eastern Australian Bushland Fae, bending down and picking up Magnot's walking stick. He held it out for the smaller man.

Magnot's face screwed up angrily, and he snatched the stick up, banging it into the dirt, and with both hands, pulled himself up to standing. Farrion observed Magnot's legs, bent at strange angles, before the dirty man pulled his brown trench coat around himself, hiding his legs self-consciously.

Magnot grimaced at the Fae King, then forced a smile, showing his yellow teeth. He tucked his long greasy hair behind his ears and patted the jacket pocket where his part of the pearl sat safely. "N-nothing, I'm out for a walk, enjoying the full moon."

Farrion's eyes moved past Magnot's shoulder toward the queen's pond before shifting back to greasy man's yellowed face.

"Why, what are *you* doing here?" said Magnot quickly.

"These are *my lands*, Magnot," said King Farrion slowly. "And it is a special night tonight, so I am patrolling the forest." Farrion shifted very slightly on his feet, making the spear glint in the light of the lantern.

Magnot began hastily shuffling away from the King. "I-I am leaving now anyway, I wasn't doing anything!"

"I doubt that very much, Magnot," said Farrion in a low voice. "But be on your way, this forest is not safe at night."

Magnot turned and scurried into the dark, and Farrion watched him leave with narrowed eyes before striding up to the queen's pond. The glass thrones sat empty, but the glowing water shifted and moved roughly, and Farrion imagined powerful mermaid tails stirring up the water as they left.

"Must've just missed them," he said quietly to himself. He would need to send a leaf-letter to Queen Tahlia to see if the meeting of the queens went well. Magnot was on the prowl tonight. And if he was anything like his sister, the witch Mankini, whatever he was up to, it wasn't any good.

ABOUT THE AUTHOR

Ektaa Bali is an emerging Australian author of fantasy fiction for all ages. This is her second middle grade novel. Find all her work at ektaabali.com and check out the Pacific Princesses website at pacificprincesses.com where you can sign up for the newsletter for exclusive updates and sneak peaks before the rest of the internet!

Printed in Great Britain
by Amazon